Freedom's Fire

Be a part of history.
Read these great Scholastic books:

ANTARCTICA

Journey to the Pole

Escape from Disaster

by Peter Lerangis

The Journal of William Thomas Emerson
A Revolutionary War Patriot

The Journal of James Edmond Pease
A Civil War Union Soldier

Freedom's Fire

J.P. Trent

AN
APPLE
PAPERBACK

SCHOLASTIC INC.
New York Toronto London Auckland Sydney
Mexico City New Delhi Hong Kong

For Martha Taylor

No part of this work may be reproduced in whole or in part, or stored in a retrieval system, or transmitted in any form or by any means, electronic, mechanical, photocopying, recording, or otherwise, without written permission of the publisher. For information regarding permission, write to Scholastic Inc., Attention: Permissions Department, 555 Broadway, New York, NY 10012.

ISBN 0-439-18926-8

12 11 10 9 8 7 6 5 4 3 2 1   0 1 2 3 4 5/0

Printed in the U.S.A.   40
First Scholastic printing, July 2000

Chapter One
April 1775

"*They*'re fighting!"

Sarah Havens straightened up from her weeding with an exasperated sigh. The twins, Hannah and Ben, were screaming excitedly and waving. If she didn't act quickly, they'd trample across the vegetable patch and ruin all of her good work. Once they were in one of their moods, all their sense went flying with the wind. "I'm coming!" she called, wiping her hands on her apron. She hurried carefully across the half-weeded bed, tucking a stray wisp of hair back under her bonnet.

Hannah and Ben were almost dancing as they reluctantly waited for her on the pathway. They were absolutely dying to tell their tale and get someone into trouble. They reveled in seeing other people in

1

hot water — it made a change from being there themselves.

Reaching them at last, Sarah looked down at the two scamps. "Now, what's going on?" she asked.

"It's Thomas and Daniel!" the twins said. As they did so often, they managed to speak together, so it sounded like one voice with a slight echo.

"They're fighting behind the barn," Hannah added, with the insufferable righteousness of someone who knows *she's* doing no wrong.

"And getting *filthy*," added Ben, since he was scolded more for that than for anything else.

"*Boys,*" Sarah groaned. "Come along." She didn't really want the twins underfoot, but she knew they'd want to watch, whether she allowed it or not. She marched off toward the barn, pausing only to pick up a bucket of well water as she passed.

Her older brother Thomas was generally well behaved — for a boy — but when he and Daniel Allison got together, there was always trouble. Both of them were quite opinionated, and each detested the other. Sarah had to admit that Daniel was hard to take, but she couldn't see why Thomas seemed to go out of his way to provoke him. Daniel was 17, and Thomas only 15, but they were pretty much the same size and build. Add in tempers that frayed quickly, and the two boys were too alike to get along well.

Sarah was tempted to let them fight and get this out of their systems, but she knew that Mother would not approve. And Mother would certainly find out, because the twins would head there next if they didn't get satisfaction from Sarah. Mother had enough to do, so Sarah would have to handle the boys.

Joshua, of course, should by rights handle this. With Father dead, Joshua was the man of the farm. But he was off in town, trading for household needs. Besides, Joshua disliked Daniel even more than Thomas did, and would probably favor letting Thomas beat the senses out of him.

Rounding the barn, Sarah almost ran into the goat, who was foraging as always. Catching herself before she slopped out too much water from the bucket, she skirted the creature, who acted as if the farm were hers by right, as she always did. Sarah glared at the two boys, who were oblivious to everything around them. They were in the dirt, scuffling and snarling at each other as they traded blows and kicks. Thomas might be getting the better of it, but it was hard to tell. It seemed more noise and motion than actual fighting, but some of the punches had to hurt.

"See?" the twins asked, smug in their own innocence and anticipating retribution on those foolish enough to fight.

"Yes," Sarah said grimly. Holding the bucket carefully, she stepped over to where the boys writhed on the ground, each trying to get the other in a headlock. Weighing the moment, she finally upended the dirty water on the pair of them.

"Wha — ?" spluttered Daniel.

"You . . ." gasped Thomas, wiping his soggy hair from his eyes. He glared up at his sister. "What was that for?"

"What do you think?" she snapped back at him, dropping the bucket with a thud. "You're supposed to be helping with the chores, not scuffling in the muck like a savage. Stop it immediately, and behave yourself." Glancing at Daniel, she added, "Both of you."

"You can't tell me what to do, Sarah Havens," Daniel growled. Nevertheless, he did seem to have lost interest in the fight. He got to his feet, dripping, and scowled at her. "You're a bossy shrew, that's your problem."

4

"Don't call my sister names," Thomas warned, getting to his feet. He looked ready to begin trading punches once again.

Sarah had colored at Daniel's insult, but she refused to take the bait. "Don't you have work of your own to do?" she asked him. "Or is your father happy to have you off the farm?"

"I was on my way there," Daniel said sullenly.

"I wasn't aware that our barn was on the path to your farm," Sarah replied. "But please let your feet keep going in the right direction." She crossed her arms and stared hard at him. As always, he looked uncomfortable around her. He wanted to say something else. Instead, he contented himself with one last glower at her, and an even dirtier look at Thomas. Then he turned to go.

To add a final insult, Hannah was there, holding his dirty cap. "You forgot this," she said, beaming at him. She enjoyed watching him take soggy steps. Without a word, he snatched the cap from her hand, crammed it on his head, and stormed away. Hannah giggled and looked at Ben, who was laughing.

"Weren't you two supposed to be slopping the pigs?" Sarah asked them.

"We were almost done," Ben protested, serious now.

"Then it won't take you long to finish, will it?" Sarah pointed out. "Get along with you both."

"Daniel's right," Hannah muttered. "You *are* a bossy shrew." She and Ben giggled at the insult, and then fled before Sarah could think of anything to yell after them.

Instead, she turned back to her brother. She had to bite back a smile, because he was quite a sight. "I think perhaps you'd better change your shirt before you do any more work," she suggested. "And dry your hair." She didn't see any point in scolding him for fighting; he already knew what she thought of common brawling.

"I was only defending your good name," he told her.

Sarah raised an eyebrow. "Oh? And now my name must be helped along by your fists? Do you think that will make me happy?"

"That's not it." Thomas squirmed uncomfortably. "Daniel said that he'd sooner have his brother marry an Indian than wed a Havens."

That brought the color to Sarah's cheeks, as Thomas clearly knew it would. It was no secret to anyone in the neighborhood that Sarah knew she had caught the eye of Daniel's younger brother,

Robert. "And so you thought to prove it a good match by beating some sense into him?" she inquired sharply. "I'm sure that improved his opinion of me greatly."

"Don't be so sour, Sarah," Thomas begged. "You know how fond I am of you, and listening to that ninny calling you names was more than I could take."

Sarah felt her mood softening. Thomas was speaking truthfully enough — he *was* very fond of her. And she could see how he had been provoked. At the same time, though, she knew that if she weakened, it would only encourage him to fight Daniel again. "All you've achieved is to make sure he only calls me names behind your back," she pointed out. "You know what Daniel is like — once he decides on a course of action, he plows ahead like an angry bull. You won't turn him around with either your words or your fists."

"Do you expect me to simply ignore him, then?" Thomas asked, sulkily.

"No. As with any bull, I expect you to simply get out of his way and let him work off his anger. Then, perhaps, he'll listen to reason."

"Daniel Allison's not on speaking terms with reason," Thomas grumbled. "If you ever wed Robert, it will be over Daniel's strenuous objections and hearty curses."

"I'm sure I can tolerate those," Sarah answered. "Boys!" She shook her head. "Why do you always have to complicate people's lives? Always fussing and fighting, and expecting us women to settle matters in your wake."

"Well, not all fighting is our fault," Thomas answered. Then, turning his head, he shouted, "Hello!"

Sarah followed his gaze and saw what had roused him from his gloom. By their house stood a coach. The horses were still attached, which showed that their visitor didn't anticipate staying long. But any visitor was always of interest.

"An important person," Thomas pointed out eagerly. "That's a fine coach." Thomas knew about such things. All Sarah knew was that coaches were wonderful to ride in, to show your wealth and importance. They couldn't afford one themselves. The farm did well, but never that well. Sarah could see the workmanship on the coach was good, probably Boston manufacture.

"Carrying someone who can afford not to ride horseback," she agreed.

"Or unable," Thomas suggested. He was quite excited now as they drew close to the house. "Come on, let's see who it is."

"Have you forgotten your appearance?" Sarah asked him. "I think Mother would prefer it if you changed your shirt and combed your hair before greeting a guest."

Thomas grimaced, but nodded. They both entered the house through the kitchen, and Thomas shot off to his room to change. Sarah stopped by the door to the parlor to check that she looked presentable, hearing the low tones of voices on the other side of the door. She rapped softly and entered the room.

Mother looked up from her chair and smiled. "Ah, Sarah. You're just in time, as always. Could you please get some tea for Mister Franklin?"

Seated opposite her mother, in Father's old chair, Benjamin Franklin nodded to Sarah. "As long as it's a Dutch blend," he commented. "Nothing English for me." Then he beamed. "I declare, Rebecca, that girl gets prettier each time I see her. The boys swarm around her like flies around molasses, I'll wager." Sarah blushed at the compliment.

"There's only one she has an eye for," Mother commented.

Franklin nodded. "She's what? Fourteen now? A good age to marry — if she finds a good man. And with her sense, and your caution, I'm sure that will be the case."

Mother cast a look at Sarah. "I'm sure you're enjoying all of this flattery, young lady, but while you are standing there, Mister Franklin is dying of thirst."

Sarah blushed deeper. With a nod, she fled back into the kitchen to prepare refreshment for her mother and their guest.

Chapter Two

*T*homas hurried to change into a different shirt, and then slicked back his hair. There wasn't time to dry it, not if he wanted to see who their visitor was. There was no telling how long the person would stay. If only Sarah hadn't interfered in the fight! But then, he realized, he'd still be out working, and not have known anyone had come calling.

Sarah should understand and sympathize with him a little more. She couldn't seem to understand that you had to stomp down hard on the kind of talk that Daniel Allison spread. It was all very well for her to pretend that it didn't matter, but the truth was that it did. If people started to believe Daniel's lies, then Sarah would be lucky to marry *any* man, least of all someone she'd chosen to wed. She might end up like Virginia McMahan, who'd been wed at 16 to a man of 53. True, Virginia had a nice house, but she had a husband who could hardly walk. It wasn't the kind of life Thomas wanted to see Sarah stuck in. And it could happen.

Anyway, there were grander things to think about these days than just marrying, and settling down, and having babies. There was independence! Now, *that* was something to stir the blood. To be free of the arbitrary rule of the English King George, and of his tame pet Parliament. That was a cause to fight for!

If only he could . . .

Satisfied that Mother wouldn't scold him, Thomas hurried to the parlor, barely tapping on the door before entering, hoping with all his heart that their visitor was —

"Mister Franklin!" he exclaimed happily. "You're back!"

"Yes, I was aware of that," Franklin agreed dryly. But his eyes sparkled behind his spectacles. "Though not officially, so I'd appreciate your keeping the news to yourself. And work seems to have agreed with you, Thomas. You've filled out into a fine young man. I only wish it agreed as well with me. The only portion of my old body that ever seems to fill out these days is my belly." He patted it and smiled.

"You've been eating too well in England, it would seem," Mother commented fondly. "All those meals with the nobility, I imagine."

"You may imagine what you will, dear lady," Franklin said. "But some of what I was offered there stuck badly in my throat." Thomas realized he was talking more of his reception than of food. "They offered me bitter things for my poor palate."

"And what are you aiming to do now, Ben?" asked Mother.

He sighed. "What else am I ever asked to do but listen and talk? I'm on my way to Philadelphia, Rebecca, where there's to be another of those dreary conventions. It's always the same — every man must say his piece and ignore the advice of his elders. And I'm the eldest there by far, so I'm ignored more than most."

"I'm sure it's not that bad."

"Only because you have never attended one of those congresses, madam. If you did, you'd be sure of nothing after two days of such debates." He shook his head. "Everyone there is far too fond of his own voice and opinion, and I'm one of the worst sinners of all in that respect, I confess."

At that moment the door opened and Sarah came in, quite demurely for once, carrying a tray of tea things, including the best silver pot. It had been a gift to their father from Paul Revere, the noted Boston silversmith, and Sarah only brought it out on the best occasions. There were only two cups, of course, for Mother and Mr. Franklin.

"Ah," Mother said, "refreshment. Are you sure you cannot stay for supper, Ben?"

"My stomach would thank me for it, but those who await me would not. I regret I shall have to put off that pleasure." He accepted the cup from Sarah, and heaped sugar into it. He stirred absentmindedly. "I can only stay long enough to ask a favor of your family, Rebecca, and to drink this tea. Then — "

He broke off as the door opened once more. This time it was the twins. They burst into the room like a minor explosion, with cries of "Uncle Ben!" Franklin put down his teacup hastily, as if expecting to be under siege any second.

"Children!" Mother exclaimed sharply. The twins quieted down instantly, realizing they had forgotten their manners in their excitement. This was, after all, only the second time they had seen Mr. Franklin, and young Ben had been named for the man.

"It's quite all right," Franklin said. "For a moment, with all that noise, I had thought myself back before Parliament."

"What was England like, Uncle Ben?" demanded Hannah.

"Did you see the *king?*" asked Ben, in awe.

"A good deal more than I wished," Franklin answered. "I saw lords and ladies, prime ministers, and a goodly collection of dunderheads. I saw people in great finery and others in great misery. Unlike our Colonies, England is a land where people are separated by their wealth — or lack of it. And it looks to me as if the English king wishes to remake our Colonies in the image of England."

"The taxes, you mean," Thomas said hotly.

"Aye, the taxes," Franklin agreed. He shook his head. "I tried to tell them that it was wrong to tax our tea to help the East India Company out of its financial messes, but they would not listen. The company has brought much of the far-off continent of India under the reach of Britain, and the government there will not allow it to fail. So we, it seems, must buy their tea — and at such an expense."

"*Our* tea is pure smuggled Dutch," Sarah said, rather proudly. "No English tea in this house."

"Well spoken!" Franklin said approvingly.

"We should dump all English tea in New York

harbor," Ben suggested. "Like they did in Boston!"

Franklin chuckled. "Yes. There was a fine joke going about in my circles in England while I was there. 'How do they make a pot of tea in the Colonies? First find a harbor.' It didn't, I fear, make Parliament smile."

It did, however, make Thomas laugh. "They'll learn not to mess with us," he prophesied.

Franklin sighed and shook his head. "I'm afraid that Parliament doesn't have that much sense, my boy. They seem to be spoiling for a fight, and it looks like a fight is what they shall have."

Thomas felt his excitement rising. "Then there will be trouble?" he asked, eagerly.

"That is certain, I'm sorry to say." The old man sighed again. Then he looked sharply at Sarah. "Unlike your siblings, you don't seem to approve of this news."

"How can I approve?" asked Sarah hotly. She looked faintly embarrassed, Thomas was pleased to see. "What is it with men, that they must solve all of their problems with fists or guns?"

"A good question," Franklin answered her. "But sometimes it seems that there are no other ways, and this is one of them. I've exhausted myself trying to speak peace, and the British king and his Parliament will have none of it. They are determined to make slaves of us — as strongly as any man over here makes an African a slave. And we cannot stand for that."

"Don't listen to her, Mister Franklin," Thomas said, annoyed. "She's just a girl, and does not understand these matters."

Franklin gave Thomas a scowl through his glasses. "There is nothing wrong with girls, Thomas. Many have as fine or finer brains than any number of men by my reckoning. And your sister has a very good point — it is a shame that we must resort to violence and arms to have our voice heard. I dearly wish that the British would hear the voice of reason, but it is too late for that." His voice softened again. "We should always wish that reason will prevail — but where it will not, then the force of the man with God's right on his side must be relied upon. And we have the right in this matter."

Mother spoke up for the first time in a while. "Then it has come to war?"

"Undeclared, as yet," Franklin answered, "but nonetheless war. When Parliament and her foolish king force British troops onto American soil, there is no other reply possible than to repel them. And our hot-tempered friends in Boston, like Samuel Adams, intend to do just that."

"And all because of taxes?" asked Sarah.

"Taxes are a small part of it," Franklin explained. "The British government also wishes to limit the lands that we in the Colonies may own. We are not to cross the Alleghenies, we are told, and yet they allow the Canadians to do as they wish. We need room to grow, and our growth scares the mother country. They see that we are strong and growing stronger, and like a bad parent, they are afraid of their child. So they try to cuff us and control us and show us who is boss. But we are of an age now to make our own decisions about our future. We do not need and cannot tolerate the laws for our people to be made and enforced by people who do not know us, and do not care to know us. They will not listen when we speak, so they will have to listen when we fight."

This was what Thomas had been longing to hear. Holding his head up proudly, he said, "I am ready to fight, Mister Franklin."

Franklin smiled, somewhat sadly. "I'm sure you are, Thomas," he agreed. "But I do not think that it is at this time appropriate."

It was as if Thomas had been punched unexpectedly in the stomach. His pride and strength seemed to flow from him. "But I *wish* to fight!" he protested. "I want to make our country free."

"And that's a fine sentiment," Franklin answered, ignoring Sarah's scornful huff of breath. "But I am here to ask your mother to lend me her eldest son, and cannot possibly take both of her strengths from her in one day."

"Joshua?" said Mother sharply. "You want him to fight?"

"Not fight, no," Franklin replied. He waved a hand. "I cannot get around as much as I wish, and I am still attempting to be the voice of reason, even in a land where reason seems unminded. But I cannot do this without accurate information. That is what I'm doing here while I am officially still voyaging home. Your Joshua is an excellent rider, and as reliable as any man I know. I wish him to act as a liaison between myself, stuck out in Philadelphia, and my friends in Boston. I would have him carry letters and intelligences, not bear arms."

This seemed to mollify Mother slightly, but it didn't settle Thomas's disappointment. "And what about me?" he asked bitterly.

"This farm must still be worked," Franklin said

gently. "And your mother and sisters — and Ben!" he added hastily, seeing a squall in the young twin's face, "cannot do it alone. You must stay and help them to keep the farm going. Our soldiers will need grain and food if they are to resist the British, for I am certain we shall be blockaded, with no supplies allowed to land."

That made Mother smile slightly. "Then I fear we shall be allowed no British tea. And they shall lose all the taxes."

"A great shame," agreed Franklin, his eyes twinkling with humor.

Thomas felt none of their amusement. "And I must stay here and turn the soil and weed the ground instead of helping free my country?" he demanded angrily.

"We all must do what tasks are assigned us," Franklin said.

"Isn't that what the British king tells us?" Thomas asked. "And *we* rebel."

"*We* are not all children," Mother said a little sharply, annoyed that Thomas was showing such disrespect. But Thomas no longer cared; his disappointment was too great. Couldn't they see how *ready* he was to fight? How good and reliable he would be?

"I am *not* a child," he replied tartly. "I am fifteen, and old enough to fight if I choose. It's not fair of you to make me stay here when such grand things are happening."

"War is never grand, Thomas," Franklin replied. "It is sometimes necessary, and often forced upon us. We should never think it grand."

"But it *is* grand!" Thomas protested. "We are fighting for our right to be free. And I have to stay home and milk the cows!" Anger and loss mingled, too strongly for him to bear. To miss out on such a grand adventure — how could he possibly endure it?

Chapter Three

Robert Allison straightened up from the row of tobacco he'd been weeding, and massaged his aching back. He was just wondering whether he could justify heading back to the house for a cup of cider when he spotted his older brother Daniel returning. It looked as though he'd been to the Havens farm, which didn't make a lot of sense. Daniel made no secret of his dislike for the family. Why would he visit them, then?

Robert couldn't understand Daniel's attitude — he'd always liked the Havens family himself, and rather more than liked pretty Sarah. He found himself thinking of her more and more lately. She was not merely pretty — though that helped! — she was also a strong worker, with a mind of her own. Daniel's opinion was that girls shouldn't be allowed to think, and that it was a waste of time. Robert, however, saw nothing wrong with listening to the opinions of anyone who could prove that her mind was active. And sometimes girls made a lot of sense — Sarah especially.

As Daniel drew closer, Robert could see why he'd been to the Havenses' — there was a bruise on his cheek, and dried blood by his left ear. He also looked as if he'd fallen into a river. "You've been fighting," Robert accused his older brother.

"I was provoked," Daniel snapped back, trying to sound dignified. "Those Havenses are just plain dirt."

"Aye?" Robert answered, grinning. "Well, it looks like some of their dirt rubbed off onto your clothing. You'd better get to work to justify it, or change before Father sees you like that. You were supposed to be going into town on an errand, as I recall."

Daniel glared at him. "I think Father will be more interested in my news than in the state of my clothing," he said. "I saw that trouble-making Benjamin Franklin leave the Havens place."

Robert frowned. Franklin had been an ambassador for the Colonies to the English Parliament for a number of years, but he had spoken only for those people who favored unrest. The man had a good reputation that Father and Daniel insisted was undeserved, and Robert could see why. Even Franklin's own son, the Royal Governor of New Jersey, had taken a stand against his father's radical views. The man was strongly in favor of independence, which was an absurd and treasonous notion. The Colonies were British through and through, and would always stay that way. Only radicals and troublemakers thought otherwise.

"What would he want at the Havens farm?" Robert asked.

"Vultures always feast together," Daniel answered darkly. "There's trouble brewing, you mark my words. Anyway, I'm off to tell Father. He and Mister Rankine will no doubt find the news of interest." He started to move off, and then said, as if by afterthought, "And if you know what's good for you, Robert, you'll stay away from that Havens girl."

"Sarah?" Robert's cheeks burned just thinking about her. He knew his fondness for her was no secret. "Why? She has no rebel leanings herself."

"She's from a tainted family," Daniel said, clearly striving for patience. It never came easy to him. "And blood will tell. If her brothers are traitors, she'll be a traitor, also."

"She has no treason in her," Robert said hotly. "I've spoken with her often enough."

"Too often." Daniel moved back and placed a hand on Robert's shoulder. "Look, Robert, I know she's a fetching thing, but she's only a girl. There are plenty of others as pretty as Sarah Havens. Becky Morrison, for one. Spend your time with her if it's a little romance you're after."

"Aye, and share her with six other lads," Robert muttered stubbornly. "It's Sarah that I like, Daniel, and no other girl."

Daniel gave him an odd look. "Liking the wrong people at this time could get you into trouble," he warned.

"What is that supposed to mean?"

"Just what I said." Daniel considered for a moment. "Mister Rankine is forming a Vigilance Committee, Robert. I'm thinking of joining it, and so should you."

"A Vigilance Committee?" That was the first Robert had heard of such a thing. "To do what?"

"To protect the right," Daniel answered. "The Havenses aren't the only potential traitors around these parts, you know. They're all stirring up emotions, and itching for a fight. Well, some of us right-thinking men aim to teach them a lesson. To show them the sort of trouble they can get into if they try to cause resentment and rebellion."

"I don't understand."

"They're like children," Daniel said. "They have to be shown that they're wrong. Their actions will only hurt themselves and others. If these traitors stir up a general rebellion in the Colonies, you know it doesn't stand a chance of succeeding. England has the largest army in the world. Why, right now one thousand men have joined General Gage in Boston to help root out the snakes there. And in a month or so, there could be thousands more arriving. And against them, the traitors can field only a handful of poorly trained militia! Think of it, Robert! If the rebels have their way, they'd have us take on the whole British Army — and that would result in the destruction of our way of life."

"And what would this Vigilance Committee of Mister Rankine's do about it?" asked Robert. He could understand and agree with Daniel's point of view, but the connection was still missing.

"We would search out those who sympathize with the rebels," Daniel explained. "And we would show them the error of their ways. Give them a taste of what might happen to us all if their ideas took firm root, instead of being weeded out as they rightfully should be."

Robert shook his head. "I hardly think that such men would listen to the voice of reason," he objected. "I've heard some of the talk, and their beliefs run deep."

"We wouldn't *talk*. We would *act*. If they won't listen to good sense, then they had better listen to a good fist or a good club."

Robert was shocked. "You'd *beat* them?"

"I'd beat any foolish child who was intent on causing trouble," Daniel said. "We've both had thrashings in our times, Robert, and it was for our own good. Traitors are points of infection, like a blight in the crop. If you don't root it out and destroy it, then it will spread and ruin the entire field. These people are just the same. If we don't stop them now, their poison will spread and ruin our Colonies. At worst, they will force the English to send troops here to subjugate us. And why should we want that? We're loyal to the Crown and Parliament, and need no soldiers to make us love our king. So we intend to move now, before the situation gets out of hand. And you should join us." He scowled. "There's already been talk about you, with you seeing that Havens girl. That's why I said you should stop. Don't let people think you're a traitor, too."

"I'm no traitor!" Robert yelled angrily.

"Then join us, and show that your heart is in the right place," Daniel urged. "Then there will be no more talk about you."

Gossip, pure and simple, Robert realized. Because he liked a girl whose family was seen as questionable, that made him questionable, also. What should he do about it? Maybe Daniel was right, but Robert couldn't see himself as part of this Vigilance Committee. It seemed to him that it was more than it sounded, and less than it was supposed to be. "I'll think about it," he promised his brother. "But I'd better get back to weeding, else Father will be annoyed."

Daniel clapped a hand on his brother's shoulder. "You're a good boy, Robert," he said cheerily. "In spite of your weakness for a well-turned ankle. I'm sure you'll make the right decision." He strode off, filled with his own self-importance.

Robert watched him go, and then returned wearily to his knees. Mechanically, he started to work, but his mind was churning with too many thoughts and emotions. Was Daniel right? Should he show people he was a loyalist? He was committed to the cause, but he wasn't sure that the Vigilance Committee was the best means to achieve that cause. Beating sense into people hardly ever worked. Look at Daniel! All the fights he'd been in hadn't taught him a thing.

Daniel had suggested that Becky Morrison was a safer choice for a wife, and perhaps he was right. Becky was handsome enough, but . . . well, she was kind of slow-witted. And she didn't have that spark of fire that often lit Sarah's eyes. Sarah was passionate about her life, and it showed in all she did. Becky was simply . . . complacent. She drifted, while Sarah soared.

But if seeing Sarah would get him into trouble, would it be a good move? Or was he betraying her by thinking like that? Was it just fear of this Vigilance Committee that made him waver? There was nothing wrong with Sarah herself— Robert was certain she had no interest at all in politics. She was no more a traitor than the ground he stood on. Both were English to their core. Giving her up simply to silence gossip would be an act of cowardice.

He wouldn't do it.

But he would have to speak with her, to be sure he was right.

And it probably wouldn't hurt to keep an eye open for this Vigilance Committee. . . .

Chapter Four

Sarah was annoyed, and she wasn't entirely certain why. As she helped her mother prepare the supper, her mind wasn't fully on her chores. It was a warm April day, and the heat from the fireplace made the work uncomfortable.

Mr. Franklin had gone on, and Mother had promised him that she would ask Joshua about riding dispatches. Sarah was sure Joshua would jump at the chance to help out. It was just like a boy to want to play war! But she was worried for Joshua, too. After all, even if he wasn't involved in any actual fighting, there was still the chance of his being arrested and thrown into jail on some British ship in Boston harbor.

Why did men have to cause so much trouble in this world? Their pride and posturing, their demands and conditions, their freedom-or-death attitudes! It was all nonsense, interfering with the business of *real* life: loving and marrying and raising a family. If it came to the rebellion that Mr. Franklin was predicting, everything would be disrupted — farming, homes, and relationships. There was talk of forming a militia group, and Sarah knew Joshua was involved in that. She'd seen her brother carefully oiling and checking his musket, and she knew his powder bag and shot pouch were full. It wouldn't take much to get him to pick them up and use them.

To do what? To shoot at some poor British soldier who was hardly to blame for any of this tension. And to be shot in return, and perhaps wounded.

Perhaps killed . . .

Sarah wondered: Did it really make any difference whether Parliament made the laws here or whether the Colonists themselves did the job? Life would go on in either event, and the rule-making would be relegated to the unimportance it deserved.

All Sarah wanted out of her life was to marry, settle down, and raise a family of her own. As her parents had done, and their parents, and their grandparents. Why did people insist on complicating life when it was really so simple?

"I think you've chopped those greens quite enough, Sarah," her mother said, a slight smile on her lips. "They're likely to boil away to nothing if you cut them any finer."

Sarah blinked, and looked down at her work. Her mother was right; Sarah had been too absorbed in her thoughts to notice. She hastily scooped the vegetables into a pot and placed it over the fire to start cooking.

"What's on your mind?" Mother asked gently. "All of this talk of rebellion?"

"Yes." Sarah bit at her lower lip, and then asked, "Why can't life be simple?"

Mother laughed, somewhat bitterly. "I wish I knew, child. But it rarely is."

"All this silly talk of fighting," Sarah protested. "People will get hurt, and for *what*?"

"I think our freedom is perhaps worth fighting for," Mother said mildly. "Could you get some sugar ready for the tea, please?"

Sarah went to the cupboard and took out the cone of cane sugar. She chipped at it, flaking off chunks to sweeten the tea. "Freedom from *what*?" she objected. "Freedom *for* what? Whatever happens, we'll still be cooking and spinning and sewing, won't we? None of that will change."

"It *would* change," her mother assured her. "What is at stake here is whether we do these things for ourselves, or for some far-off masters whose only interest in our Colonies is in how many taxes they can squeeze out of us." She patted Sarah on the shoulder. "You're worried about your brothers, aren't you? That they will be forced to go and fight?"

"Yes," admitted Sarah, though that was only one of her problems. "They could be hurt. They could be *killed.*"

"I know that." Mother looked haunted. "And I knew that when your father marched off with the militia to fight in the Indian Wars. He didn't want to go, especially because you were all much younger then and unable to help around the farm. He hated leaving me to do everything, even with my brother's help. But he knew that he had to protect our land, and our lives, so he went. And I was terrified for him. I was afraid I'd never see him again, that he'd be killed and . . . mutilated by some savage in the woods. I feared you would all grow up never knowing your father. They were the worst months of my life. But then he came back, and I thought things would return to normal and life would be happy again." She sighed. "And it was, until the accident." Mother looked at Sarah. "I don't want to have to see my sons go off to fight, either. But I'd sooner they fight and even die than for us to be governed by tyrants."

"Tyrants?" Sarah shook her head. "It's only lately you call King George and Parliament that. While Mister Franklin was in England, you had a higher opinion of them. Perhaps you listen too much to his opinions."

Mother frowned. "While he was there, there was still a chance that they might listen to sense. Now it is clear that they do not want reason. They wish to show us who is in charge of these Colonies. Well, I think it's time that we showed them. And I do not think they will like that demonstration."

"People will be injured and killed in the showing," Sarah replied. "And they will be people we know. Perhaps even members of our family." *Perhaps even Robert . . .*

"Believe me, Sarah, I know that. And it sits in my heart like a large, cold stone. But we cannot allow our personal fears to rule in our lives. There are greater things at stake than our lives."

"What could be greater than that?" asked Sarah bitterly. "All of this nonsense is ruining my life!"

"Ah . . ." Mother nodded as though she had finally understood something. "So that's what this is really all about, is it? Our people are confronting the British king solely to ruin your life? Sarah, I'm rather disappointed in you. I had thought you were capable of a little more thought for others."

"Why?" Sarah snapped. "Nobody seems to be thinking of *me*! All I want is a quiet life. How could that be possible with all of this talk of fighting?"

"The problem here, Sarah," Mother said, "is that it's all reduced down to what you want. And life is never all about the dreams and desires of any one person. You must start to see the larger picture."

"You're starting to sound like a man!" Sarah exclaimed. "*Larger picture!* What could be larger for any of us than a home and family?"

"A country?" her mother suggested.

"We are not a country," Sarah replied bitterly. "We are thirteen Colonies of *England*."

"For the moment, certainly. But that may yet change. And so, too, I hope, will your thinking." Mother took the chopped sugar from her. "I'm not sure I should leave you working with a knife. You seem to be taking out your anger on our poor supply of food." She turned to check on the ham. "Sarah, none of us really *wants* conflict. But it would be foolish of us to pretend it will not happen. And even more foolish not to prepare to win. And if that means that you can't marry Robert Allison this fall as you had planned, then so be it. The sun will not rise and set as you wish it, and neither will the affairs of men. Like women through all ages, you must learn that your wishes and the ways of the world are often in collision. Please consider that you may have to suspend your own desires for a while in the cause of something greater." Sarah started to open her mouth, but Mother held up a hand. "And that is all we shall say about the matter until you've had time to think about it. I don't enjoy hearing all about your selfish desires, especially in such a time of crisis."

Sarah blushed furiously at being scolded, but she knew better than to argue the point. Mother was rock-firm when she made a decision. Sarah would simply have to hold all of her thoughts inside her until she could talk with someone more sympathetic. Since Mother had made her own sacrifices in her life, she clearly expected Sarah to do the same — and to somehow enjoy the experience.

Joshua arrived home shortly before supper. He and Thomas unloaded the packages from the cart, and then fed the horse before they washed up for supper. Sarah helped to serve the food, smacking the hands of both twins as they attempted to take too much sugar. They both had a sweet tooth, and would leave nothing for the rest of the family if they could get away with it. The family was all settled and eating the ham before Joshua brought up the subject that they were all clearly thinking about.

"Thomas told me that Mister Franklin was here today." He smiled slightly. "I think he managed to remember everything that was said. I understand that Mister Franklin wishes me to work for him as a messenger."

"That's right." Mother was clearly striving to act as if this were a normal dinner conversation, but Sarah could read the tension in every line of her face. Mother had to be going through a terrible strain. Sarah admired her mother, but at the same time wished that she would simply forbid Joshua to do anything so foolish.

Joshua nodded. "I can start first thing in the morning, if that is all right with you, Mother," he said casually. "Thomas can take over my chores, especially if Sarah can help out a little. You'll hardly even know I'm gone."

"I'm sure we'll all notice that," Mother said. She was trying to smile. "Take care of yourself, Joshua."

"It's just carrying messages," he said carefully. "I won't be doing any fighting, I'm sure."

"You'd better take your musket just the same," Mother suggested.

"Of course."

If he wasn't fighting, why would he need the musket? That didn't make any sense to Sarah. And how could Mother have suggested such a thing? Surely she didn't want Joshua to get hurt? It took all of Sarah's willpower not to yell at them both for being so foolish.

Thomas, however, wasn't as strong. "It's not fair!" he exclaimed.

Mother looked at him mildly. "Life often isn't fair, Thomas, and you should never expect it to be. Finish your supper."

He pushed the plate away from him. "I can't eat," he snapped.

"You'd better eat," Joshua warned him. "You'll need all your strength with the extra work to do."

"I don't want to work," Thomas said sulkily. "I want to go with you and fight."

"That's out of the question," Mother said firmly. "With Joshua gone, we'll need your help around the farm even more than usual. Sarah, the twins, and I can't manage this place on our own."

"Fighting for our freedom is more important than helping out here," Thomas argued stubbornly.

"No, it isn't," Joshua said. "Would you want to see Mother and the others starve while you're off having some grand adventure? If we both go, that's what would happen. What's the point of fighting for our country's freedom if you condemn your own family to a slow death?"

Thomas wasn't giving in so easily, though. "Can't you get help from the neighbors?" he asked. He glared at Sarah. "I'm sure *she* could get Robert Allison to pitch in — he'd do anything for her."

"You know we can't afford to pay for help," Mother said. "If we could, I'd have done it long ago, so you all could have had more time for your schooling. I know it's hard for you, Thomas, but I'm afraid you have no choice. You must stay here with your family and help us run the farm. And that is my last word on the subject."

Thomas opened his mouth to object, but Joshua leaned forward. "The answer won't change, Thomas, because the reasons won't change. You can't go, and that's all. I'm sorry you don't understand, but if you think about it, you will. Eventually."

Thomas jumped to his feet. "It's not fair!" he

cried. "It's just not!" He whirled and ran from the room.

"That was very rude of him," Hannah said primly, acting as if she were the very model of good behavior.

"You should punish him," added Ben, helping himself to the meat from Thomas's plate. When he saw Sarah's glare, he shrugged. "No sense in wasting it, if Thomas isn't going to eat."

Nothing, it seemed, was going to make the twins change. Not even the possibility of war. Sarah sighed. This was all foolishness, and she wished it was all over. The boys were already thinking of fighting and glory, but not of suffering and death. Neither of them had a single lick of sense between them. If it were up to her, she would forbid *both* of them to go. Was she the only sane person left?

Chapter Five

*T*he following morning didn't improve Thomas's mood. He was up before the sun, as always, and determined to do his work dutifully. If he had to stay behind, forced to do farm chores instead of fighting for liberty — well, nobody would say he shirked his responsibilities. He was dressed and out of the room he shared with Joshua before his older brother was even awake. He took a quick drink of cider, and then went out to the barn to begin milking.

Joshua found him there a short while later. "Maybe you should let up a little on your anger," his older brother suggested. "I think you're hurting the poor cows."

"They'll get used to it," Thomas said coldly. "If I can, they can."

"Cows are just dumb animals, Thomas," Joshua

said. "They accept what they must because they can't do anything else. I'm sorry you can't come along, but this is how it must be. The sooner you accept that, the happier you'll be."

"Really? And isn't that the argument that England is using on us? That we must accept what is going on, and the sooner we do, the better we'll be?"

Joshua sighed. "I can see that you're determined to act like a martyr. Well, I'm sure you'll tire of the role soon enough." He crossed to one of the mares, Freya, and began to saddle her. She was the most reliable, if not the fastest, and on a trip such as this, reliability would be more important than speed. It was the horse Thomas would have taken.

Thomas felt a momentary twisting in his stomach as he watched his brother prepare to leave the farm. For how long? Would he even come back again? Still hurting from the betrayal he felt, Thomas steeled himself and carried on with his chores. Who cares *what* Joshua did? Let him go off and play the hero, forcing Thomas to stay behind and play the farmer. Who cares?

Watching out of the corner of his eye, Thomas saw Joshua finish his preparations by slinging on the bag of provisions and a pouch containing the letters of authority that Mr. Franklin had left behind. Then he strapped on his musket and the bag of balls and powder. As Joshua clambered into the saddle, Thomas heard the chink of coins; Mr. Franklin had left a small amount of money to help defray Joshua's expenses, knowing that the Havens family could spare little themselves. It was at this moment that Thomas realized that Joshua was indeed leaving on his adventure.

He felt sick at heart.

Joshua patted Freya, murmuring encouraging words into her velvet ear. Then he looked down to his brother. "Thomas, you're the man here now," he said. "Whatever your personal feelings, remember that. You're the one Mother will look to for help and strength. Don't let the hurt inside you spill out. She needs you to be strong and supportive."

"I can be anything she needs," Thomas said coldly. "I have to be, don't I? It's my place in the world."

"Please, Thomas, be a man, not a child." Joshua leaned down and offered his brother his hand. "Till we meet again, eh?"

Thomas turned away. "You'd best be going," he suggested. "It's a long ride to Boston, and if you linger any longer, it'll be sunset."

Joshua hesitated a moment, and then he rode away. Standing outside the barn, Thomas was determined not to look. It was so unfair! But then he couldn't help himself — his brother was leaving, perhaps never to return. He spun around, wishing he had said something to Joshua that wasn't bitter. But it was too late for that now. He saw the far-off figure on horseback pull off his hat and wave it. Thomas almost waved back until he heard the voices of the twins, and realized that Joshua was waving to them and not to him. Soon Joshua was gone, lost in the morning mist and distance.

"Isn't it exciting?" Hannah asked, hurrying toward Thomas. She'd forgotten her bonnet in her excitement and her hair was unbound.

"There are chores to be done," Thomas growled, letting the anger and disappointment take over again. "Do you think the pigs will feed themselves?"

"Ben will," Hannah giggled, watching as Ben hurried up, chewing on a lump of bread. "But I suppose we have to do the others." To her twin she snapped, "Come on!"

"You're sounding just as bossy as Sarah," Ben complained, spraying bread crumbs as he talked. "What's wrong with all the women in this family?" But he followed along toward the wallow.

What indeed? Thomas had been wondering that himself. Why couldn't any of them be sensible? He set back to work, trying to put Joshua out of his mind. To be stuck here, when all of the action was elsewhere . . . It was too much to bear.

The next hour or so kept him too busy to do more than nurse his resentment as he turned the cows loose to pasture, checked that the twins had taken care of the pigs properly, and started them on feeding the chickens while he collected the eggs. By the time that he took the eggs and the milk to the house, Sarah and Mother had breakfast cooking. But even the delicious aromas couldn't break his mood.

Sarah, as always, was completely oblivious to his feelings. She was always lost in her own world, which could be very annoying. "Didn't Joshua look handsome as he rode off?" she asked him.

"He looked much the same as ever," Thomas snapped. "Only his head was perhaps a little more swollen with self-pride than normal. Then again, you seem to like boys with too much pride."

"There's no call to be so grumpy," Sarah retorted. "If you ask me, you're lucky. This is all simple foolishness."

"Nobody asked you," Thomas growled. "And you

think anything but billing and cooing is foolish. *Oh, Robert!*" he mocked her.

"Just because no girl will look at you," Sarah scoffed. "You'd have a mighty different opinion of romance if *you* saw a pretty face smile at you."

"I think that's quite enough," Mother said firmly. "I know our emotions are all running high this morning, but there's no cause for all of this bickering. Thomas, would you please fetch the twins, so that we can have breakfast together? And please bear in mind, both of you, that I would prefer that we all be polite to one another."

"Yes, Mother," Thomas replied. He had fallen back into his obedient servant role. He'd do whatever he was asked to do, and endure his suffering unobserved. The twins were happy, as ever, to stop working and come in for food. Both of them were pretending to sword fight as they did so. Thomas, six years older, could scoff at their childish ideas of war. Everyone knew that if there was war with England, the fighting would be with guns. The British might manage to field more men, but the Americans would have men who grew up using muskets for hunting and for self-defense.

The day wore on slowly. No matter how hard he tried to get through it, it seemed as if the hours were mired in the mud he was working in. All he wanted was for it to be over, so he could go to bed and forget this day. And all the rest to come.

Eventually, the light started to fade. He drove the cattle back into the barn for the night, checked that the twins had finished their chores, and went back to the house. His stomach was rumbling, but he could hardly bear the thought of food. Supper was prolonged, and he managed to stay silent throughout, save for a few mumbles when Mother asked questions about the farm.

After the table was cleared, the pewter plates scraped, and the dishes sanded and washed, they all went in to the parlor. Mother seemed to be determined to act as if this was simply an ordinary day. "Sarah," she said, "I think it's time that you did more work on your sampler."

"Do I have to?" Sarah asked plaintively. She was only a moderate seamstress, and hated working on the family tree.

"All young ladies must do their sampler," Mother said primly. "Get out your basket, and set to work. Twins, get your books. I want to hear you both reading."

"I'm going to be a farmer," Ben objected. "Why do I need to read?"

"How will you know if you've enough food to last the winter if you can't keep track?" Mother asked.

"I'll get my wife to do it," Ben said, grinning.

"You'll be luckier than Thomas if any girl will look at you," Sarah commented. She'd managed to prick her finger threading her needle, and it hadn't improved her temper.

"Well, we all know who looks at *you*," Hannah crowed. "Robert Allison!"

"That's none of your business," Sarah snapped, flushing. Why she should be so sensitive about such common knowledge was beyond Thomas's understanding. Or caring.

"The Allisons are a good family," Mother said sternly. "It would not be a bad thing to be wed into such stock. Sarah shows reasonable good taste."

Thomas couldn't stomach this any longer. "Mother," he objected, "they're *loyalists*. They support the British against the Colonies! How can you even *think* about any one of us marrying any one of them?"

"Robert is *not* a loyalist!" Sarah exclaimed. "And if he is, so what? What difference does it make, anyway? Loyalist or rebel, he's a man with a strong back and a good spirit."

"Mother!" exclaimed Thomas. "Tell her she's not to even think about marrying into the Allisons!"

"I hardly think that's your business," Sarah snapped.

"Children!" Mother said sternly. "That's quite enough! Thomas, apply yourself to the spinet. I think you need the practice."

"Aren't you going to tell her?" demanded Thomas, reluctantly taking his seat. He wasn't in the mood to play music tonight, but he *had* decided that he'd do whatever he was told.

"What words I have on the subject of your sister's marriage, young man, are between myself and her." Mother fixed him with a grim stare. "You worry about your own life. Now, play. We could use a little music to lift our spirits."

Thomas opened his *Playford's Dancing Master* at random, and started to hit the keys savagely. The result was hardly musical, but he didn't care.

"I knew you'd be on my side, Mother," Sarah said smugly. She was embroidering the tree itself now, apparently more at ease.

"I hardly said that, young lady." Mother sat back, closing her eyes. She was obviously savoring the scent of the bayberry candles that lit the room.

That always relaxed her, because they normally used the cheaper tallow candles. "I said that we would have words, but now is not the time." She glanced at the twins, who were attempting to look completely innocent and failing miserably. "But later — we shall have to talk."

For the first time that day, Thomas felt a slight touch of satisfaction. Self-righteous Sarah was getting a taste of being told what to do. And she clearly didn't like it. Good! It was about time somebody else hurt like he did.

Chapter Six

The past few days had been terrible for Robert. He'd been kept busy on the farm, but his mind was constantly on Sarah. He'd been unable to get away to see her, but he needed to talk with her. He had so many questions and so many doubts, which he needed to resolve. His father, however, had refused to let him leave the farm. He'd given no explanation, but Father rarely did. He simply issued commands, and expected them to be obeyed without question. Sometimes Robert felt as though he was being treated like a hired hand rather than the second son of the house.

Today was Sunday, and that made a big difference. As he dressed in his best clothing for church, Robert knew he'd at least have a chance of seeing Sarah. Everyone went to church, unless there was illness in the family. He was sure he'd get a moment to speak with her, whatever happened.

Daniel was still in a good mood. He'd been to see Mr. Rankine twice, with Father's approval. There was still a lot of talk about the unrest that looked to be coming to a head in Boston. The New Englanders seemed determined to cause trouble. It was known that their bands of militia were storing stocks of gunpowder and bullets. This wasn't exactly illegal, but it didn't look right. Especially when coupled with the rebellious nature of the men of the Boston area. That business with throwing the tea into the harbor had caused plenty of conflict, and it didn't look to be dying down.

But that had little enough to do with Robert and even less to do with Sarah. The British troops under General Gage would deal with that handful of malcontents, and order would be restored. Life would go on, and Robert had decided that he was going to do something about his own life for a change.

Of course, he hadn't actually told Father yet. . . .

They set out for church together. It was a fine morning, so Father decided that they would walk the two miles. This was fine with Robert, as it gave him the time to compose his thoughts. What was he going to say to Sarah? What was the best way to get her to listen? He was almost certain of the reception he'd receive, but *almost certain* was hardly good enough. . . .

As they neared the church, the bells were pealing. There were a few buggies hitched close by, but most people had walked. Robert scanned the crowd as they approached the building, but he couldn't see Sarah or her family. That was disappointing, but he could wait until after the service. Father strode down the aisle to their pew, opening the gate so that they could go in. Robert glanced around as they sat, and his spirits rose as he caught sight of a pretty bonnet in the Havenses' pew on the other side of the aisle. Sarah was here!

"Eyes to the front, boy," his father growled in a low, stern voice. "This is the house of the Lord, remember, not some vulgar tavern."

Shamed, Robert turned his eyes forward again. His hands clutched his hymnal tightly. It was sheer torture not to be able to turn and smile at Sarah. But Father was right—he was here to worship God first. Affairs of the heart could wait for later.

Robert stumbled through the opening hymn, and then Mr. Hayes rose. The rector led them all in a second hymn and a prayer, on which Robert could scarcely keep his mind. Then Mr. Hayes moved to the pulpit, opening the thick, leather-bound Bible.

"I shall take as my text this day," he intoned in his rich bass voice, "the twenty-fourth chapter of the book of Matthew, starting with the sixth verse." He adjusted his spectacles, looked down, and began to read:

"And ye shall hear of wars and rumours of wars: see that ye be not troubled: for all *these things* must come to pass, but the end is not yet.

For nation shall rise up against nation, and kingdom against kingdom: and there shall be famines, and pestilences, and earthquakes, in divers places.

All these *are* the beginning of sorrows."

Abruptly, Mr. Hayes slammed the book closed, which made everyone jump. He stared out at the congregation, as an owl stares at a mouse he's sighted as prey.

"And, I tell you, we are at the beginning of sorrows. In our day, in our time, we are seeing nation rising up against nation — and we are one of those nations. There can be none in this body who is unaware of what is happening in New England. Though some think it will not affect us, I tell you here and now that it can do nothing else." He stared around the room, as if daring anyone to contradict him. "And what is the response of a Christian to such events?" he asked. "I shall tell you!"

And tell them he did — for almost two hours, Mr. Hayes talked and talked. He moved from "render unto Caesar that which is Caesar's" to "fight the good fight." Robert found it hard to pay attention, and almost impossible to decide whether the rector was for or against the king. Still, it kept Father and Daniel transfixed, and Robert stole a moment to look across the aisle. He was rewarded in two different ways: First, he saw Sarah smile back at him; second, a swift clip to his ear made his head ring. Robert turned back to pretend to pay attention to the sermon, but his mind wasn't on it. He kept seeing only Sarah's smiling face. . . .

Eventually, even Mr. Hayes ran out of energy. He'd once talked for three hours without a break, so this was one of his shorter sermons. After a closing hymn and a final prayer, church was dismissed. Robert wished he could dash out, but he knew that Father would never abide such a display of emotion. Meekly, he filed out behind Daniel. He did see that

Sarah was just ahead of them, though, and was sure she'd find some way to hold back a little and give him a chance to catch up to her.

Outside, the day was warm and cheery, with a slight breeze. People were in no hurry to rush off, and were stopping to chat with one another.

"I must speak with Mister Hayes," Father said abruptly, and he moved to join the knot of people around the rector. No doubt Father would either congratulate him or complain about the sermon; He was notorious for handing out his opinions. Daniel scurried after him, so Robert took the opportunity to look around.

Sarah looked as if she was attempting to edge away from her family. Mrs. Havens was conversing in a low voice with Mrs. Van de Water, and the two families were slightly intermingled. Robert moved closer, his heart pounding. Sarah, who had been glancing around urgently, caught sight of him and moved slowly away from the group to meet him.

Now that he was with her again, Robert had lost the thread of what he had planned to say. "That's a lovely bonnet," he stammered, hardly daring to look into her deep green eyes.

"Thank you," Sarah murmured. "You, too, look handsome."

Robert glanced around, wondering how long they would have together. He screwed together all of his courage. "I have to speak with you," he said urgently.

"You *are* speaking with me," Sarah pointed out.

"Not like this," he said. "Alone! Today."

Sarah nodded. "At six? The lightning-struck pine?"

She'd obviously been thinking the same thing, and had only been teasing him. "Yes," he agreed, relieved. "I have something to ask you. . . ." That was as far as both his courage and his time could take him.

"Robert!" That was his father's stern voice. Robert whirled around, embarrassed again. "Come here!"

Robert didn't even dare wish Sarah good-bye. Instead, he sped to join his father and Daniel. His older brother smirked at him.

"You shouldn't talk to filth," Daniel offered.

Robert's face burned red. "She's not filth!"

Father stared coldly at him. "That family is known to harbor treasonous views," he stated. "I will not have my sons associating with the likes of them."

Father's voice carried far. Mrs. Havens obviously

heard him, for she turned around, away from her conversation, and fixed Robert's father with her own cold gaze.

"If you wish to insult me, Mister Allison," she said, "perhaps you would have the courage to do it to my face and not my back."

"If I wished to insult you, madam," Father replied, "then I should make certain you heard me. As it was, I simply mentioned that you are known to harbor treasonous views. If that is an insult, you have my apology. I had believed it to be a simple fact."

"Treason?" Mrs. Havens asked, raising one eyebrow. "Perhaps to a man whose tongue is black from licking the boots of his British masters, the desire to be free would seem to be treasonous. But to those of us who choose to stand tall, the word seems inappropriate."

There were more than a few cheers at this, and Robert saw his father's face color with anger. "Aye, but a dog who turns on his master should be beaten and not encouraged."

"Perhaps *you* are a dog, fawning over the king's few scratches behind your ears, but I am a woman, and an American one at that. I have no master, nor does any free person." Mrs. Havens glared at him proudly.

"Please, neighbors!" Mr. Hayes said worriedly, moving between them. "Remember, this is the Lord's day. We should have Christian charity toward one another."

Robert's father gave the rector a cold glare. "I am filled with Christian charity," he said slowly. "Toward other Christians. But one could hardly call a woman who scorns her God-appointed king a Christian."

"And one could hardly hold that a man who supports tyrants is a Christian, either," Mrs. Havens retorted. "So it would seem that there is little call for charity — which should well suit your mean-spiritedness, Mister Allison."

That made Robert's father color further with anger. "If you were a man, madam, I would demand satisfaction from you in a duel!"

Mrs. Havens raised an eyebrow. "And if *you* were a man, I might accept." She deliberately turned her back on him. "Come, children, I think the air around here is getting thick with the poisonous stench of a loyalist." She hurried the family away. Sarah cast one agonized look back before she was forced to leave.

Robert was completely at a loss. It looked as though his father and Sarah's mother were about to start their own private war. With that being the case, what would happen next?

Father was furious, but he would never allow himself to lose his temper publicly. He would wait till he was home again to do that. Heaven help the hand who gave him any cause for anger today! Robert knew he'd best keep quiet and immediately obey anything his father said. "That family is vermin," Father hissed. "Come!" Whirling on his heels, he strode away.

As he did so, Mr. Rankine moved to join them. He was a tall, muscular man, respected rather than liked, and a confidant of Robert's father and older brother. "You spoke well, Charles," he murmured. "Don't let that woman affect you. She and hers will get their due when Parliament crushes their traitorous aims."

"I'm not sure I can wait that long," Father responded darkly. "Parliament, after all, does not live next door to her, and I do."

"You may not have to wait," Mr. Rankine said. He glanced around. "I'll be over to see you in private, and we can talk. Perhaps the time has come to teach a few of the folks around here that we are still loyal to our king." He nodded, and moved off.

This comment disturbed Robert. Daniel had

mentioned that Mr. Rankine was forming a Vigilance Committee, and it seemed as though he might be ready to move. What did he have in mind? And how would it affect matters between Sarah and himself?

Sarah! Robert felt a rush at the thought that he was to meet her that evening. But he knew that he dared not mention her name to his father at this moment. The public row would not help Robert's case. There had to be something he could do to win over his father, but Robert didn't have any clue as to what it might be.

Would he have to give up all hope of marrying Sarah Havens? How could he ever do that?

Chapter Seven

Sarah was burning with humiliation as she hurried home in her mother's wake. How could Mother have done such an awful thing? Arguing with Mr. Allison — and in public like that! It was quite scandalous, and Sarah knew she'd never be able to show her face in town again without being thought of as a shrew's daughter.

But she knew better than to take her mother to task for that public spectacle. Mother was convinced that she was right, and she had a stubborn set to her face. Even the twins were quiet, not wishing to attract Mother's anger in their own direction. Thomas actually looked proud of Mother — which was not too surprising. Thomas hated the Allisons and enjoyed seeing them publicly embarrassed.

Sarah was so ashamed, she hung her head. What would Robert think of her now, after that disgusting exhibition? He probably hated her and all of her family. How could Mother have ruined her life like that? Sarah wished she could just curl up somewhere and die. Instead, she walked dutifully along behind her mother, all the way home.

Several people had even tried to congratulate Mother, but at least she had simply brushed them off — politely, of course — and continued toward home.

"That was telling him!" Thomas crowed, once they were on the road to the farm. "You were wonderful, Mother!"

"I should not have done it," Mother said, although she still looked proud of herself. "The Allisons have always been good enough neighbors, even if they do support the king."

"He *asked* for it, and you gave it to him," Thomas protested.

"Perhaps so," Mother agreed. "But I should not have done it so publicly. Charles Allison is a proud man, and he is bound to be annoyed."

"Let him be," Thomas said airily. "Who cares about the hurt feelings of a loyalist? When we free ourselves, he'll be in trouble."

"You should always care about the feelings of others," Mother corrected him. Sarah could hardly believe the hypocrisy of those words! Mother hadn't shown any concern at all for Sarah's feelings. "Just because they do not hold the same opinions as yourself doesn't mean that other people are either fools or scoundrels. It is possible to disagree politely."

"The Allisons aren't polite," Thomas objected.

"All the more reason for you to be, then. It will show them up far worse." Mother glanced at Sarah. "You're very quiet, which is hardly usual for you. Don't you have any opinions on my behavior? Or are you learning wisdom at last and keeping them to yourself?"

"I could have died from embarrassment," Sarah said honestly. "How could you have *done* that?"

There was a touch of red in her mother's cheeks. "It was done in anger, and I regret it. But it *was* done, and must be lived with. I hardly think I've lowered anyone's opinion of myself. And I doubt you'll be scarred by my words, either."

"You forget, Mother," Ben said slyly, "that she's soft on Robert Allison." Sarah felt like slapping him around the ears for that remark, but knew it would only annoy Mother if she did.

"So I had," Mother agreed with a slight smile. She shook her head. "You think he won't like you now, Sarah? If that is so, then the boy's a fool, and you're better off without him."

"How can you *say* that?" Sarah demanded. "You insulted his father in public — of *course* he's going to hate me for it."

"Anyone who'd hate you for what I did is a clod," Mother answered. "And I wouldn't have you marry a clod. If you think that of him, then you'd best stop thinking about him and set your sights on some other boy."

"I don't want any other boy," Sarah protested.

"That's as well," Mother said. "You're probably too young to wed, anyway."

"I'm *fourteen*!"

"I am aware of that." A smile tugged at her mother's mouth. "And once *I* was fourteen and desperate to be married before I became an old maid. And not that long ago, either. I know how you feel."

"How?" demanded Sarah. "Did your mother insult your chosen's father in public, too?"

"No, my mother always loved your father as if he were her own son." Mother placed a hand on Sarah's shoulder. "And I think Robert Allison is too generous a soul to hold my failings against you."

"He doesn't even hold *your* failings against

you, Sarah," Thomas put in with a grin. "If he can tolerate your bossiness, I'm sure he can bear anything."

"You don't understand, either of you!" Sarah exclaimed.

"I understand more than you think," Mother said gently. "I assume those words you had with him after church were to arrange a meeting?"

Sarah blushed. Had she been that obvious? "Yes. But I'm sure he won't show up after what you did."

"If he doesn't show up, that will tell you something about his character," Mother said. "I don't approve of his father, but I've nothing against the boy himself. I see no reason why you shouldn't meet with him — *if* he has the courage to show up." Mother gave her a penetrating stare. "And I'm sure I don't need to remind you to behave like a young lady."

Sarah flushed. "Of course I will!"

"Good."

Ben and Hannah started giggling. "Sarah's got a beau!" they chorused.

"And you two will have thick ears if you don't watch out," Sarah snapped. That only made them giggle even louder, until a glance from Mother quieted them.

Mother seemed to think that she'd somehow resolved the problem. She obviously didn't understand *anything*. But at least one of Sarah's fears had been crushed. She'd been afraid that Mother would forbid her to meet with Robert. But Mother always prided herself on being fair, even when she wasn't, and she clearly was trying to make it look as if she was open-minded about Robert. Sarah had no idea how true that was.

Time dragged by until it was late enough for Sarah to excuse herself from the house and make her way across the farm to the lightning-struck tree. All the way, Sarah's stomach hurt. Would Robert show up? Or would he hate her now? Every step of the way was agony and fear. So much could have been lost. . . .

Her heart quickened with excitement as she realized that there was a figure beside the tree. Her pace sped up, and she had to force herself to remember her dignity or she would have run to meet Robert. He was looking out for her, and when he spotted her, he waved and came toward her. They met halfway, Sarah struggling not to look out of breath.

"I was afraid you wouldn't come," Robert said, his own breathing rather fast from his hurrying. "After this morning . . ." He rolled his eyes.

"I know," Sarah agreed. "I could have *died*! It was so horrible. I was afraid *you* wouldn't be here."

"Nothing can keep me from you, Sarah," he promised.

Sarah felt so filled with happinesss at this profession of love that she felt it would shine from her, like light from the sun. "Oh, Robert!"

He swallowed. "I've been thinking," he said, "and I know . . ." He broke off, flustered. "Oh, I don't know how to say this! I've practiced and thought about it, and nothing is coming out right."

"Just say it, then," Sarah suggested, hardly daring to breathe. Was this what she'd been hoping for?

Robert nodded, and took a grip on his runaway emotions. "Sarah Havens, would you do me the honor of becoming my wife?"

Sarah fought hard to contain her own emotions, knowing she should behave like a lady at all times. But it was so difficult! "Robert Allision, I would be the one honored to call you *husband*."

He grinned widely at that, and let his breath out explosively. "I was so afraid you'd say no, or laugh at me," he confessed.

"And *I* was so afraid you wouldn't want me after what my mother did," Sarah admitted.

"Well, I know you don't feel the same way that

68

she does, so how could I blame you?" He took both of her hands, and a tingle went through her entire body at his touch. "But it does, of course, complicate matters."

That brought her down to earth again. After everything, more problems. "How so?" she asked anxiously.

"Well, I am only fifteen and you fourteen," Robert explained. "We shall need our parents' consent to wed. And, knowing how they feel about each other . . ." His voice trailed off.

Sarah's joy completely evaporated. "And they will never give it, you fear?" She thought about what Mother had said earlier. "I shall speak to my mother," she vowed. "I think that she might be persuaded. She dislikes your father, but thinks herself too fair to be prejudiced against you for it. She may give her consent."

"May." Robert obviously thought it too fragile a word for his hopes. "And I shall speak to my father. I confess, though, that I am not at all certain of a favorable response."

Sarah nodded dully. She feared the same. But the question must be asked, and they would have to live with matters, however they turned out. Forcing down her dread, she clasped Robert's fingers. "We shall have to pray that God will soften both of their hearts. If they love us, they will consider our happiness first before coming to a decision."

He nodded, attempting to take courage from her words. "I will try. We shall meet again, whatever happens."

"Yes." Sarah sighed. "This is both the brightest and stormiest day of my life. I am honored and happy that you have asked me to marry you. And I am frightened about what may happen next."

"I feel exactly the same way," Robert admitted. "But we must be brave, if we are to win each other." He hesitated, and then asked nervously, "May I kiss you, now that we are engaged to wed?"

Sarah remembered her mother's warning about being always a lady. But she and Robert *were* engaged — at least for the moment — and they were hardly in public, where someone might be scandalized. "You may," she breathed.

He leaned forward clumsily and pressed his lips to hers. Sarah shut her eyes, savoring the touch. It wasn't quite what she had ever imagined, but it was still a thrill. Robert Allison, kissing her! Then he pulled back, obviously flustered, and let her hands drop.

"I had best be going," he said.

"Yes," she agreed, though she would rather have him stay. But they had to talk with their parents, and that would not be easy for either of them. Still, the sooner it was done, the better it would be. At least then they would know.

"I'll meet you here tomorrow?" he suggested.

"Yes." Sarah nodded and half turned. "I shall pray we are both successful. I love you, Robert."

"And I you, Sarah," he said, red in the face. "Good-bye." He waved slightly, then turned and dashed away.

Sarah stood, watching him, holding her hand to her pounding heart. He had asked her! It was what she had been hoping and wishing for, and yet there were still obstacles in their path. If only she could know how their parents would take this. . . .

Chapter Eight

Joshua was leading Freya through the darkness, toward the small points of light he could see ahead. He wasn't sure how late it was, but it had to be past ten, and he was both hungry and tired. He was still making his way north toward Boston and believed he was in the southern part of Massachusetts. He was regretting his decision not to stop at the last town he'd passed through, believing he'd find another before night fell. He'd proven to be very mistaken, and darkness had caught him on this miserable track that was supposed to be a road. Not wishing to risk Freya, he'd been forced to dismount and lead her the past couple of miles. Now, at least, there were some small lights ahead, which meant either a farm or a town.

As he drew closer, he saw it was actually a village, hardly more than a couple of dozen houses, bunched together around the church like chicks around a mother hen. Joshua glanced around, not wishing to disturb any sleeping inhabitants to ask for shelter. There was evidence of candlelight from a couple of houses, but what he really needed was an inn — if a place this small had one.

To his relief, it did. A two-story building had a candle lit and placed in a prominent upper window. This was the unmistakable sign of an inn. As he drew closer to the building, Joshua saw that there was a battered sign hanging above the door, proclaiming it to be DUNNE'S INN. There was no other sign of life, however. Taking up a small handful of gravel — positioned close to the door for just such a use — Joshua threw it lightly against the window with the candle. This was so that only the innkeeper would be wakened; banging on the front door would rouse the whole place.

After a few moments, the door slowly opened, and a yawning man in his mid-fifties blinked out at Joshua. "It's late," he commented.

Joshua was tempted to point out that he was well aware of the fact, but he didn't want to annoy the man further. "I'm sorry. The towns in this area are a little farther apart than I'd expected."

"Not a local, obviously." The man eyed Freya.

"Best tie her up around the back. I'll open the kitchen door for you. I can only give you cold mutton, bread, and cheese if you're hungry."

"That sounds wonderful," Joshua assured him honestly. "I won't be long." As he turned to lead Freya, he heard the door close behind him. There was enough light from the moon for him to pick his way to the back of the inn, where there was a small enclosure for horses. It held three already, along with a measure of food and a trough. Freya slipped in gratefully to join them. Joshua took the saddle and his bags with him to the inn.

As promised, the kitchen door was open, and the innkeeper was carving from a small mutton roast. A slab of bread, a piece of cheese, and a cup of cider already waited on the table, and Joshua fell to with thanks.

"Where are you headed?" his host asked, passing over several slices of meat. It was a little fatty but delicious.

"Boston," Joshua answered. He'd prepared a story in case he was asked; he couldn't tell the truth, since there was no way of knowing whether his host was a loyalist or rebel sympathizer. "I'm off to see a silversmith named Revere."

"You've picked a curious time to travel there,"

the man replied. Was it just idle chatter or something more?

"The troubles, you mean?" Joshua shrugged. "Well, it's my own fault. It's my parents' wedding anniversary in a few weeks, and I wanted to get them a nice gift. Revere made them a coffee set for their wedding, and I thought a matching tray would be perfect. Of course, I've left it late, what with the farm chores, and I realized that with the troubles, Boston might soon be difficult to reach."

"That's for sure," the innkeeper agreed. "These cursed rebels are causing trouble everywhere, it seems. They're bad for business." He scowled. "You'll have to share a bed tonight, though — I'm full up."

"That will be fine," Joshua assured him. So the man was a loyalist. A good thing Joshua hadn't told him the truth! And he didn't seem to see anything odd in saying that the rebels were bad for business, but that he was full up.

"Good. Up the stairs, the room on the right." The man nodded to him. "Breakfast is early, so don't sleep in."

"I won't," Joshua promised. The man lingered, so Joshua reached into his pouch for the price of the meal and bed. Satisfied his guest wouldn't leave without paying, the man went back to his own bed. He left a candle burning so that Joshua could finish his meal. Once he was done, Joshua took the candleholder and ascended the stairs. He opened the door on the right and saw that the innkeeper had been telling the truth. The room here ran the length of the house, and there were three beds in it. Two already had three men in each, and the third had only two. Just enough room, if he wasn't fussy. But after all the riding he'd done, Joshua was glad just to be able to lie down. Quietly, he placed his saddle beside the bed, removed his shoes, and then snubbed the candle.

As he lay down, he heard the sounds of snoring. The hazards of travel, he knew. Well, he was tired enough to sleep through even a barrage of English guns, so this shouldn't be a problem. . . . Taking up as much of the quilt as he could, he closed his eyes. . . .

Thomas had to admit that he found his mother's behavior hard to understand.

"Robert seems like a decent boy," she said. "Unless I know something against him, I won't forbid him to woo Sarah."

"Mother, he's a *loyalist!*" Thomas objected.

"I have not heard him say so," Mother replied. "Certainly his father and brother are, but that does not make Robert one."

"Trust me, he is."

She patted his hand. "I do trust you, Thomas. But I must hear it from the boy himself, and not as gossip. And even if he does support the king — that hardly makes him our enemy, does it?"

"What else can he be?" Thomas was so frustrated with her! How could she talk like that?

"Thomas, many people in the Colonies support King George and Parliament. We cannot insist on fighting all of them as well as the English troops. Whether they like it or not, they are Americans, also, and we must treat them as such."

"They would not be so generous with us," Thomas objected.

"I have told you before that you must never judge yourself by what you see others do," Mother chided him. "You must always know that what you are doing is right, even if others are acting badly. If they do wrong, then it is on their heads; you must strive always to do that which you know is right. Do not sink to their level."

"All right, Mother."

She smiled fondly. "I hope that you mean that,

and aren't simply saying it to make me happy." She shook her head. "Besides, you know your sister — do you think that my forbidding her from seeing Robert would make her stop?"

Thomas had to snort. "It's not likely. She's too mule-headed to do as she is told."

"Then let's not tempt her into disobedience by forbidding her what she thinks she desires."

Thomas caught the words with interest. "Then you believe she's not really in love with Robert Allison?"

"I have no idea," Mother said. "And I suspect that she doesn't, either. She's fourteen, and at her age, girls want to be in love so badly that sometimes they convince themselves that they are when they are not. But then again, some girls *are* in love at fourteen. I know I was, and my love was quite real." She smiled. "The five of you would not be here now if it were not true. So I don't know." She gave him an amused glance. "And when am I to hear that you wish to wed, also? You're the same age as Robert Allison, and not, I think, unattractive to the girls."

Thomas found himself blushing. "I've no interest in romance," he told her. "All that concerns me at this time is the struggle for freedom." Seeing the sharp look in her eyes, he added hastily, "And, of course, doing my farm chores."

"Well, perhaps you should have your eye out for some suitable woman," Mother said. "You'd be less likely to want to rush off and have your head blown from your shoulders if there was some girl who would rather have it resting in her lap."

Thomas blushed deeper at the thought. True, some of the girls in church were quite fetching . . . but he had other concerns. One silly-headed romantic in the family was enough. "Shouldn't you have told that to Joshua?" he asked, hoping to get off the hook.

"I have mentioned it to him once or twice." Another smile. "Or a hundred times. But he feels as you do — that this is not the time to wed and have children, with such troubles as are on our horizon. And perhaps he is right." Mother looked around. "Where are the twins? They're being quiet, which usually means they're doing something wrong and don't want to be discovered at it."

"They did say they were going to check on the pigs," Thomas answered. "They seem convinced that old Susie is going to give birth any moment, and they each want to lay claim to their own piglets."

Mother smiled. "Well, the pigs can look after themselves, even with the twins around." There was a sound from the stoop, and then the door opened. Sarah, looking rather flustered, came in. "A short meeting, I see," Mother commented. "Obviously he showed up, or you'd still be there waiting."

"Yes, Robert was there," Sarah agreed. Her face was flushed, and it wasn't from rushing. "We talked."

"As long as that's all you did," Mother commented. "And did you talk *about* anything?"

"He — he asked me to marry him," Sarah blurted out. Thomas rolled his eyes in disgust. It was just what he had feared.

"Did he now?" Mother looked interested. "And how did you reply?"

"I accepted," Sarah answered, looking half excited and half scared.

"Ah! I assume that Robert remembered that you're both in need of parental permission to wed," Mother commented. "You seem to be lacking the practicality to think of it."

"Yes, he did," Sarah admitted.

"Well, that's another mark in his favor." Mother sat up straight in her chair. "And how does he propose to support you?"

Sarah looked blank. "Support me?"

"Yes, child," Mother said. "Support you. Or did you imagine that once you were married you could live on air and dwell in the forests like savages? How will he support you?"

"We . . . we didn't discuss that."

"As I expected. You're filled up with your emotions, leaving no room for your senses. You need a little common sense in your lives."

Thomas was careful to stay out of this, curious to see where it was going. His silly sister was all aglow with love, and hadn't thought any of this through. But how would Mother reply? If it was up to Thomas, he'd pitch a bucket of cold water over such crazy ideas. But it wasn't up to him. And Mother was proving to be quite unpredictable these days.

"But you haven't *answered* me!" Sarah protested. "Do we have your permission to wed?"

"I suspect the problem will be in getting his father's permission," Mother said. "And I don't need to answer you. Until Robert Allison comes to me to ask for your hand in marriage, there's nothing to be said."

Sarah looked as though she was about to throw one of her temper tantrums, which wouldn't be a wise move right now. Even she must have realized that, because she took a deep breath. "Then what of me?" she begged. "Can't you at least help me out of my agony?"

"I doubt it," Mother said dryly. "Young love is an agony that can't be soothed. It must either fade, or blossom into a sturdy plant. There's little I can do about it." She clearly saw how frustrated Sarah was becoming and held up a hand. "I can't answer you until I know what his intentions are. I need to know whether he is serious, and how he intends to look after you. I will not let him marry you to allow him to starve you to death because he has not considered how he may support you — and a family. So until I have talked with him, I can give you no answer."

Sarah was ready to scream. "You are the most frustrating person!"

"And I am also your mother, which gives me the right to be so. Now, I suggest that you look to your sampler again. Believe me, you will get plenty of practice for your sewing skills once you are married."

"But I don't *want* to!" Sarah snapped.

"Young lady," Mother said coldly, "I am quite tired of hearing all about what *you* want. Maturity is about understanding that other people have desires and needs also, and turning your attention to such things. Now, please remember that you are only one member of this family, and that you have your duties and responsibilities. Once you leave this house to settle with your husband, those obligations are severed. Until then, you will do as I tell you." She managed a thin smile. "And when you have a daughter of your own, you will begin to understand why I do what I do, for you will do the same with her."

Thomas snickered; it was about time that Sarah was put in her place. It was a bad move, however, because it reminded Mother that he was still in the room.

"As for you, young man," she said, "I think you had better go and rescue the pigs from the twins after all. And then you may practice your spinet. And I trust I shall not hear that *you* don't want to, either!"

"Yes, Mother. No, Mother." Thomas spun around and sped off on his errand. It was probably better to be far away from his mother right now!

Chapter Nine

*H*is heart filled with dread, Robert returned home. Though he was thrilled that Sarah had accepted his proposal, he knew that it would not be the simplest task in the world to get his father's blessing. If only his mother were still alive! She would have understood his feelings, and she could have talked to his father until he agreed. But Mother had died three years ago, along with the baby she was carrying, in a difficult birth. Since then, Father seemed to get colder and more distant each day.

The housekeeper, Mrs. Robson, met him at the door. The Allison farm was profitable enough to employ not only six hands in the fields, but also a housekeeper, a cook, and a maid. After his mother had died, Robert had dreaded the thought that his father might marry Mrs. Robson — herself a widow of ten years — and make her Robert's new mother. Thankfully, his father thought the idea even more repugnant than Robert did, and it had never happened. It hadn't stopped Mrs. Robson from hoping, though.

"There you are," she snapped. "Your father has been looking for you this past hour. Don't keep him and his guest waiting any longer." She glanced down. "And wipe those shoes before you take another step into my clean house."

Robert wanted very much to inform her that it wasn't *her* house, but this was not the time to start a row. Instead, he wondered who their guest was as he wiped his shoes on the scraper. He hurried to the parlor, and let himself in after tapping on the door.

"Ah, so there you are at last, boy," his father said, impatience clear in his voice. "Come in and close the door behind you."

Robert did as he was bidden. As he came into the room, he saw that their guest was Mr. Rankine, and that Daniel was already present and looking very pleased. This was clearly not the best moment to ask his father about Sarah Havens. "I'm sorry, Father," he apologized. "I've been walking and thinking."

"Two healthy tendencies," Mr. Rankine observed. "More boys should do both."

"But not when they are wanted in the house," Father commented. "Well, you're here now, which is what matters." He glanced at their guest. "Would you be good enough to repeat what has been discussed so far, to bring this sluggard to some form of awareness?"

"Certainly." Mr. Rankine looked at Robert. "You know, of course, that there are numerous traitors in the area who are fomenting strife and creating trouble in the Colonies with the ultimate aim of breaking free from our historic ties to England?"

"Yes, of course," Robert agreed. He wasn't really interested in discussing politics right now, but it looked as if he had no choice.

"Well, we feel that the time has come for them to learn that the majority of the people here are loyal to their king and country, and that they cannot get away with flouting the law and our wishes so easily. They hide themselves from the law, but they cannot hide from us, their fellow citizens. We are forming a Vigilance Committee, whose aim it is to root out any traitors and expose them for what they are."

Robert nodded. "That seems like a reasonable thing to do," he agreed. "Then they can be punished for their actions."

Mr. Rankine smiled broadly. "Exactly. And that is what we shall do to them. Show them that treason has a price to pay."

Robert frowned. "I thought you meant reporting them to the constable, and having the law deal with them."

"The law is too slow and uncertain," Mr. Rankine said, with conviction. "Why, any jury that tried such a man might well have his fellow sympathizers on it, and he could be acquitted. No, the Vigilance Committee will deal with any traitors itself, without recourse to the law. We shall punish them as they deserve."

This disturbed Robert, though he had to agree that juries could easily be tampered with. There were any number of people who might not be traitors themselves, but who sympathized with those who were. And in a country where free expression of one's mind was held dear, people might simply be reluctant to punish a traitor, thinking he had a right to his views, no matter how illegal. But for a group of citizens to band together and dispense justice themselves . . . It just didn't seem right to him. "And what kinds of punishment would that be?" he asked warily.

"It would depend on the level of their treason," Mr. Rankine answered. "Sometimes simply a warning will suffice, if given in a wise enough ear. Other times . . ." He shrugged. "We will use whatever it takes to convince such wretches to abandon their false beliefs and come back to loyalty to our God-appointed king."

Robert still had his doubts, but he could see that none of the other three did. His father looked grimly satisfied and Daniel eager. Mr. Rankine seemed to be earnest and committed.

"What do you say, boy?" he asked. "Will you join us?"

"To work for the Crown and the welfare of our Colonies?" Robert said. "I would be a poor citizen if I did not."

"Capital!" Mr. Rankine slapped him, rather too heartily, on the back. "Welcome to our latest member, then!" He turned to Robert's father. "Now, then, we have to decide on our first target. I had thought Hiram Clayton."

The printer? Robert knew the man vaguely from church, of course. A tall, spare man, stooped from bending over his typesetting all day. He had two young daughters and a rather plump wife.

"A good choice," Father rumbled. "The man has been printing seditious pamphlets and flyers and distributing them to stir up public opinion. It would be a service to stop his lying tongue."

Daniel grinned. "He's been preaching rebellion for years," he said. "It's about time that he got a taste of what he has been calling for, don't you think?"

Robert was still less than convinced that this was a good idea, but he could hardly deny that Mr. Clayton was both a traitor and an agitator. Stopping that stream of evil-minded literature he produced would certainly be a public service. He simply nodded his own commitment, though.

"Excellent!" Mr. Rankine beamed at them all. "I shall go along and organize the other members of the Committee. As soon as we are ready, I shall send you word. Then we shall strike a counterblow against these traitors. Long live the king!"

"Long live the king!" the Allisons all chorused. Mr. Rankine shook hands all around, and then took his leave. Daniel went with him to see to his horse, leaving Robert alone with his father. For once, Father actually looked rather cheerful, and Robert decided that the time to ask his permission would never be better.

"Father," he said gently. "I have been thinking about getting married."

His father blinked and looked at him as if he had forgotten his younger son was still in the room. "A reasonable preoccupation for a man of your age," he agreed. "I take it you speak of a girl in particular, and not simply girls in general?"

"There is one, yes," Robert admitted, his throat a little dry. His heart was pounding from nerves. "We would, of course, need your permission to get married."

"Naturally." Father looked down at him, eyes narrowed. "And, no doubt, my help in establishing a home. Do I know the girl?"

"Yes, Father." Robert winced inwardly. This was the hard part. . . . "It is Sarah Havens."

"*Havens?*" Father glowered at him. "What are you *thinking*, boy? Haven't you been *listening* to what we've been saying?"

Robert paled, and tried to control his shaking. His father was reacting worse than he had imagined possible. "Yes, but —"

"The Vigilance Committee is being formed to

root out all traitors and agitators! We have to be the hand of the king, dispensing justice and upholding the right! And then you come to me, and have the nerve to tell me that you want to marry the daughter of one of the worst of them all? How could you even *think* I could possibly agree? I'd sooner you wed the daughter of the Devil himself than any whelp of that harridan!"

"But Father," Robert protested. "Sarah isn't a traitor! She does not care at all for politics, and —"

"She is from a family of vipers, and that makes her a viper, too!" Father thundered. "If you're burning to be married, that is normal for a young man. But for the sake of heaven, choose an appropriate girl! You will *never* have my permission to wed Sarah Havens. I do not even want to hear that name mentioned in my house again!" He spun on his heel and stormed from the room.

Robert stared after him, desolate. He had expected problems with achieving his desire to marry Sarah, but even he had never imagined *this*! His father would never change his mind, and Robert's fate was sealed: He had no option but to obey, and forget Sarah forever.

If he could. . . .

He wished that he was a girl, so he could collapse and weep, but he was a man, and too strong for such weakness. He brushed at his eyes — merely irritation from the pollen — and ran to his room. He was not going to give in to his emotions, no matter what.

Chapter Ten

*C*oncord, Massachusetts Colony, was a mess when Joshua reached it. Freya had ridden well, but they were both quite tired after days on the road. He stopped a passerby and asked for Colonel James Barrett, the leader of the town's militia and one of the men for whom he had letters.

"He's at Wright's Tavern," the man answered, pointing the way. It turned out to be a two-story building with plenty of activity about it. Joshua noted a number of minutemen, of whom he had heard much. This group of militia fighters had been formed two years before, when Concord had been chosen as the meeting place for the Provincial Congress. Its name, he understood, came from the idea that they could be ready to fight at a minute's notice. It certainly looked as though they were ready to fight now.

Joshua handed over Freya's reins to a young stable hand, and then entered the tavern. The small main room was thick with smoke from all of the pipes men had lit. There was considerable noise in the room, and people were jostling and shifting about. Unsure of what to do, Joshua touched the arm of the nearest man and asked again for Colonel Barrett.

"He's over there," the man replied, gesturing to a table where a man sat going through a thick ledger. He held a quill in his ink-splattered hand. "But this isn't a good time to disturb him. The British are on the move, and it looks as though things might get rather rough."

"I'll chance his anger," Joshua said, removing the man's letter from his pouch. He managed to push through the crowd of men around the table and approach the colonel as he worked. He was a mature man, probably in his sixties, slightly younger than Mr. Franklin. He was concentrating on his book with a fierce intensity as Joshua cleared his throat and said his name.

Barrett glanced up, annoyed. "Can't you find someone else to bother?" he growled. "Or don't you see that I am busy?"

"I'm sorry, Colonel," Joshua apologized. He held out the letter he was carrying. "I'm a messenger from Mister Benjamin Franklin."

The weary face broke into a slight smile. "Old Ben? What does the scoundrel want now?" He took the letter and broke the wax seal. Joshua waited as the colonel scanned the letter swiftly. "Ha! He's after news, as always. He's too much the politician these days." He dropped the letter onto his ledger and considered for a moment. "Well, my boy, there's not much to tell him yet. But if you've the time to stay here a day or so, I'll warrant there will be news enough to please even Ben's heart. The British in Boston are preparing for action."

"Action, sir?" Joshua felt his excitement rising.

"Action," the colonel repeated, with a nod. "General Gage has had more than a thousand of his men roaming about the countryside, looking for militia and supplies."

"And a fat lot of good it did him," one of the men close by remarked. "They may as well have been chasing hobgoblins!" There was general laughter at the thought.

"Well, he isn't likely to be sitting on his backside for much longer," Colonel Barrett commented.

"Parliament is taking a dim view of his inaction, and is pressing him to take measures against us. He's assembled a force of his best troops — light infantry and grenadiers, as well as a couple of hundred Royal Marines. It's under the command of the marine Major John Pitcairn."

"You seem to know a lot about his plans," Joshua commented in amazement.

One of the other men laughed. "Boy," the man said, gesturing with the stem of his pipe, "Pitcairn has his troops assembled by the ships in Boston Harbor. He's been collecting longboats to ferry them. Half the people in Boston town can see this happening under their very noses. We'd be very poor militia indeed if we *didn't* know so much."

"But we don't know the all-important details," the colonel added. "When they will march, and what their aim will be. Pitcairn's obviously going to strike somewhere, and strike hard. Doctor Warren has a couple of riders waiting to alert us as soon as anything happens. And John Hancock and Samuel Adams are staying in the home of the Reverend Jonas Clarke in Lexington. They'll be off in a few days to join Ben Franklin and the others at the Continental Congress." He looked around the crowded room. "Where is our host? Someone rouse him, and see if there's a spare room this lad can stay in for a day or so." He glanced back at Joshua. "And, by the look of things, you could probably do with a hot meal and a drink or two. Here, Samuel — take the lad and have him seen to." One of the men nodded. "Don't come back till you're fed and rested," the colonel ordered Joshua. "Meanwhile, I've the books to finish." He picked up his quill again and bent back to work.

"This way," Samuel said, shoving aside anyone who was in the way. "It's a bit thick in here today, I know. But there's tremendous excitement building. The British will be on their way any time now."

"Aren't you afraid?" Joshua asked. He could hear laughter and boasting, but no signs of worry.

"Of them?" Samuel sniffed in scorn. "They won't do anything to us, except try to steal the supplies the colonel's laid up. He's well organized, you know. We've twenty thousand pounds of musket balls and cartridges alone, and thousands of pounds of dried fish and rice for supplies. But the colonel will see to it that the British don't get any of it."

"They won't attack you?" Joshua asked. "I'd have thought there was a danger of serious fighting."

"Serious?" Samuel snorted again. "After the Boston Massacre, they're under orders to use only powder in their guns — and they won't do a lot of damage without balls or cartridges. Anyway, there are about six thousand militiamen scattered about the countryside, and we've riders aplenty to alert them. If the British do anything, we'll have men here so fast that they'll be trounced." He winked. "You're as safe as can be here, and you may get to see some of the fun."

They had reached the kitchen now, where several young girls and one tired-looking man were cooking at the huge fireplace. There were two large hams being turned by a couple of the girls, and a huge pot of vegetables bubbling away in the embers. The scent of fresh-baked bread made Joshua salivate; he'd eaten nothing for the past day, wanting to reach Concord quickly.

"Can you supply some victuals for our young friend here?" Samuel asked the man. "He's just in from New Jersey, seeking news for the Congress."

"I've more news than food what with the way you men eat," the innkeeper grumbled. Nevertheless he looked around. "Betsy, see if you can turn up a few scraps for this stomach on legs here, will you?" He looked back at Joshua. "I hope you're not too particular about what you get."

"I eat most food, sir," Joshua replied.

"Good." The innkeeper turned back to preparing a large mutton pie. "Now leave me in peace."

"One last request," Samuel said. "Do you have a bed for the young man?"

"A bed?" The man snorted. "Every bed I own and can borrow is filled." He wrinkled his nose. "But if he has as little objection to horses as he has to scraps, I imagine he could sleep in the barn."

"That'll be fine with me," Joshua assured him.

"Good," the innkeeper replied. "It's as good as you'll get these days." He returned to his cooking.

Betsy touched Joshua's arm. She was a pretty young girl of about 14, much the same age as his sister Sarah. "This way," she said, leading him out of the confusion to the rear door. She had a pewter plate of stew and some of the marvelous-smelling fresh bread. Beside it was a pottery cup of cider. "You might do better eating outside," she suggested, handing him a spoon. "It's not likely to get any quieter or calmer in here."

Joshua could understand that. He went out the back door and found there were a couple of tables and chairs set up. There were three people already at a table, so he took one of the loose chairs, setting his drink on the ground. Digging into the food made him realize just how hungry he was, and he wolfed everything down quickly. Betsy seemed to have guessed his mood, for she brought him another slab of the bread and refilled his cider.

"Has it been like this long?" he asked her.

"For the past few days," she told him. "Everyone's expecting trouble any time now. Are you here to join in the fighting?"

"No. I'm to carry messages."

"That's probably safer."

"Samuel seems to think there's not much danger," Joshua commented. "The British aren't allowed to use musket balls, I gather."

"That doesn't prevent them from using their bayonets, or from clubbing people," Betsy pointed out. "And I imagine their ruling will be suspended if someone from our side shoots at them first." She glanced at all of the men hurrying around. "In all this excitement, I'll be very surprised if Colonel Barrett can keep everyone under his control. A lot of people are for attacking the British, you know."

"Feelings are running a lot higher here than in New Jersey," Joshua admitted.

"We've suffered from the British troops longer,"

she pointed out. "If a few thousand marines occupied New Jersey towns, I'd imagine the feelings there would be hotter, too."

"You could be right." He glanced around, seeing the frantic activity. He realized that Betsy's estimate of the men's mood was nearly correct. "It does look like people are ready for a fight."

"You're better off out of it," she informed him. "If you can stay out of it. You might be a messenger, but you must be a patriot, too. Otherwise you wouldn't be here."

Joshua considered the point. He *had* told his mother that he wouldn't fight, but it was more a comment than a promise. Mother had been intelligent enough not to seek his word on the matter, and he'd been careful not to suggest that he'd given it. He *did* have a mission. . . . But if fighting began, he also had a musket. Could he just sit and watch while others fought for freedom? Or would he feel compelled to strike his own blow?

He honestly didn't know. Accepting more cider from Betsy, he shook his head "I don't know what I'll do," he told her.

"I don't know what *any* of you will do," Betsy said. "But I'll be praying for all of you."

Joshua watched her reenter the tavern. Then he sat back, cupping his drink. He had a strong suspicion that something would be happening shortly. But would he be simply an observer — or a participant?

Chapter Eleven

Sarah's head was all awhirl. The twins were teasing her terribly, but she hardly cared. Why was Mother being so mean? She refused to give any kind of a direct answer about marriage with Robert, even though she could see how the uncertainty was hurting Sarah. Sarah had been desperate enough to actually try and enlist Thomas's help in convincing Mother to talk. She should have known better.

"I think you're crazy twice over," he answered. "First, for wanting to marry at all. Second, especially for wanting to marry an Allison."

Sarah flushed at the very thought. "I don't much care *what* you think about my marrying Robert Allison. I just want to know what *Mother* thinks!"

Thomas shrugged and returned to splitting logs for the kitchen fire. "She hasn't told me," he replied, swinging the ax. "And I'm not going to ask her. If she wanted you to know, she'd tell you." *Slam!* Two logs clattered aside, and he placed a fresh piece on the block.

"You're no help at all!" Sarah stormed.

"Well, that about matches the help *you* are around the farm at the moment." Thomas pulled out another log. "Now, I know you have chores you're neglecting, so don't let me keep you from them any longer."

"*Boys!*" Sarah huffed and walked away, even more annoyed than when she'd begun. Thomas was just making fun of her and refusing to help. And after everything she'd done for him, too! Oh, why was everybody being so beastly? It just wasn't fair!

She could think of nothing else all day. She hardly cared that her chores were being neglected. All she could think about was Robert. What was he going through? What had his father said? Had Mr. Allison been as infuriating as Mother? The whole day was pure torture for her.

Finally, though, it was near enough time to go to the lightning-struck tree again. She hurried to it, eagerly looking for signs of Robert. But this time he wasn't there. Disappointed, Sarah assumed she had simply arrived too early. She sat on the grass beside the tree, where she could look into the Allison lands, and waited.

And waited.

As time slipped by, the pain in her stomach grew worse. What was happening? It had to be past six by now. Where was Robert? Had he been forbidden to see her? Sarah wouldn't have put that past his father — the old tyrant! But surely Robert could have slipped away if he really *wanted* to. Why hadn't he come?

The longer she thought about it, the less Sarah was sure about. It was all agony, and the only way to resolve it would be when Robert came.

But he didn't come. . . .

Eventually, Sarah gave up waiting. With leaden heart and feet, she trudged back to the house. He hadn't come. It didn't really matter why; he'd let her down. Did she *really* want to marry somebody who could be that inconsiderate and unreliable? Yes, she realized, she did. She wanted Robert very badly, no matter what his reason for not keeping their rendezvous. Every step hurt her pride and her hopes and her dreams. Every step built up her worries and her fears. Was their love doomed to frustration and death? Well, if it had to be, she would bear it. She would never, ever love again, but she would remember this love, and keep it bright and fresh in her dying heart for as long as she lived.

With luck, it wouldn't be that long. She might easily catch some terrible disease and waste away and die. *That* would show them all! How would Robert feel then about failing her? How would Mother feel about her insensitivity? How would Thomas feel about his annoying teasing? They would all contribute to her death, but she wouldn't hold it against them. She'd forgive them all with her last dying breath.

It would make them feel even worse for the rest of their miserable, Sarah-less lives.

But how *could* Robert have disappointed her like this?

"Hey, Sarah!" It was the twins, playing on their swing-rope. "You're in for it now!" Ben called.

"Yes," Hannah agreed gleefully. "Mother is going to take you to the woodshed and beat the tar out of your behind for sure."

Sarah glared at them crossly. "What is the matter with you?" she snapped. "Aside from a lack of the brains God gave a goose?"

"At least *we* do our chores," Ben sneered.

"And we don't go all around the countryside

mooning over Robert Allison," added Hannah. "You've got grass stains on the back of your skirt. Were you *kissing* him?" She puckered her lips. "Mmmmmm!"

"None of your business," Sarah retorted tartly. If only she *had* been!

"You'd better go in now," Ben advised her. "Before Mother gets even madder."

Sarah tossed her head and walked on. Why would Mother be mad at her? The twins were just trying to annoy her, that was all. She marched into the house and removed her bonnet. Her hair felt kind of straggly, but she really didn't have the enthusiasm right now to brush it.

"Ah, there you are," said Mother from the kitchen. Sarah was puzzled, because Mother *did* sound cross. "You've finally recalled that you're a member of this family, have you?"

Sarah blinked. "I'm afraid I don't know what you mean."

"And I'm afraid you don't, either," Mother snapped. "It seems that no matter what I tell you, you don't listen, do you? I don't know how you could imagine that you could get away without doing your chores today, young woman. Especially now that Joshua has gone, you know we need every hand we have. I simply can't have you going off somewhere all day, woolgathering. There is too much to be done. Now, are you going to start bearing your share, or do I have to pretend that you're eight years old again, and take a switch to your backside?"

"Mother!" Sarah was shocked and embarrassed. "How could you even *think* about doing that?"

"I can promise you that I'm more than thinking about it," Mother said angrily. "The only reason I haven't done it yet is because I know you've spent the day mooning over Robert Allison's proposal. Well, I'll accept one day of foolishness for that excuse, but no more. If you don't pull your weight tomorrow, I don't care how old you are. You'll be over my knee, and Robert will have to do his wooing to you while you're standing up. Do I make myself clear?"

"No!" Sarah was on the verge of tears, almost as if she really had been switched. "Mother, how can you be so *mean* to me? Why can't you show more understanding? Why can't you be more happy for me?" One thing Mother had said suddenly sank in. "It's because you want me here on the farm, isn't it?" she demanded, conviction flooding through her. "Because Joshua isn't here, you can't spare me. And that means you're going to ruin my wedding plans, aren't you? How *could* you?"

Mother glared at her furiously. "We're not all as selfish as you, young lady! My answer to Robert will be based solely on whether I think he can look after you. If he's half as woolly-headed about this business as you are, I certainly won't give my blessing. But if he's thought it out and has plans for your future, I will consider his proposal with all seriousness. Though why any man would want a selfish, ungrateful, unthinking little bundle of tears is beyond my understanding."

"You're *hateful*!" Sarah yelled.

"And I am still your mother, so I expect some respect from you for that, at the very least. And a little understanding would help, but that would appear to be well out of your grasp at this moment."

"You could try to understand *me*!" Sarah snapped.

"I *do* understand you," Mother said coldly. "And I'm not at all sure I like what I see. I understand that you're consumed with the idea of marriage right now, but you have to moderate your attitudes. You have work to do and a family to help support. I will not allow you to neglect these responsibilities simply so you can go off with Robert Allison! I trust that you told him that I would like to see him?"

"So would I!" yelled Sarah. "He didn't meet me."

That seemed to get through to Mother. "He didn't?" she asked, with considerably less annoyance in her tone.

"No! And I'm sure you're glad about it."

"I am never glad at anything that brings my children pain," her mother replied. "I'm sorry to hear that he didn't meet you, but I'm equally certain he must have had a good reason for it."

"What could keep him away from me if he loved me?" Sarah demanded. She was on the verge of tears, she knew, but couldn't help it. "*Nobody* loves me!"

"It seems to me that *you* love yourself quite enough right now," Mother observed. "But when you're able to start thinking straight once again, you'll come to understand that. For now, it seems that theatrics and fears are going to be your response to most events. I know everything seems bad right now, but it will change, I promise you that. Perhaps not in the way you'd most like, but it will alter. Especially your perspective on these events."

She moved forward to hug Sarah, rather unexpectedly. "You have my sympathy and support, though, Sarah."

It felt good to be held, even though Mother was treating her like a child again, and not a grown woman. But she needed comfort, and would take even that. The sobs came now, as her fears and shame overtook her. Mother said nothing, merely held her and stroked her hair until she was quite worn out of tears. Sarah eventually straightened up and brushed the tears from her cheeks.

"That's better," her mother said. "I'm sure you feel better now."

"I feel *miserable*," Sarah complained.

"Well, that's a step up from where you were before. Now, I'll say no more about the missed chores today. But in the morning I expect you to remember that until — and if — Robert Allison marries you, you are still a member of the Havens household, and, as such, have duties and responsibilities. So set your personal problems aside for the time being and resume your place with us. I'm sure Robert will show up as soon as he is able."

"What if he doesn't?" asked Sarah, afraid.

"Then he's a poor human being, and you're better without him in your life, no matter how unbelievable that may appear to you right now." Mother patted her on the arm. "Now, let's see if you've any appetite left after all that bawling, shall we?"

Sarah sighed. Mother *really* didn't understand. But she did feel a little hungry right now. . . .

Chapter Twelve

Robert's stomach was churning; he felt sick. However, he had no option but to continue with the rest of the Vigilance Committee. He'd tried to escape going with them, but he had been unable. After all, he could hardly tell his father that he wanted to meet with the girl he'd been forbidden to marry.

What did Sarah think of him now? She had to be furious and disappointed with him for not meeting her as he had promised. But with Daniel sticking close by his side, Robert simply didn't have any option.

Besides, what did he have to tell her? Nothing good. *My father absolutely forbids me to marry you.* Hardly what she'd want to hear, and nothing that he wanted to say. Yet, somehow, sometime, it would have to be said. Robert wanted to vomit, but though his stomach was tying itself in knots, it refused to cooperate to make him sick enough to legitimately back out of this action.

Along with his father and brother, Mr. Rankine had assembled eight other men, all grim-faced and determined. Daniel, on the other hand, was looking as though he was enjoying himself — as he probably was. All of them carried cudgels, walking sticks, or other stout wooden implements. Robert had the handle of an ax, though he felt self-conscious and foolish with it.

"It's just a precaution," Daniel assured him. "If Clayton starts any trouble, we'll be able to stop him."

"I don't know," Robert admitted. "It looks rather menacing."

"It's *supposed* to look menacing," Daniel said, sighing in exasperation. "We've got to convince the traitor to stop printing his rebellious pamphlets and newsletters. He won't do it if we just *ask*, will he? So we have to show him that he'll be in for trouble if he doesn't behave himself."

Robert could see the logic in that, but he wasn't at all happy with it. "I thought one of the things the Vigilance Committee was against is the kind of public violence that the rebels have been doing. Isn't this the same thing?"

"Yes," Daniel agreed, grinning. "A taste of their medicine is clearly what's called for here." He tapped the palm of his left hand with the walking stick. "They're so fond of violence and uprising, let's see how *they* like it when it's done against them."

"But that doesn't make us any better than they are," Robert objected.

"Of course it does!" Daniel looked at him as if he were a dull-witted two-year-old. "We're in the right, defending the natural order of things. They're rebels against their lawful, God-given monarch. Honestly, Robert, if you can't see that, you're more hopeless than I imagined."

"I can see that," Robert answered. "And it's why I agreed to help the Vigilance Committee. I'm just not sure that violence is the right response here."

"Well, nothing else makes sense to them!" Daniel snapped, his patience clearly tested. "Do you honestly think that Clayton will stop publishing his lies if we just *ask* him? No, we have to *tell* him. So stop acting like a little girl, and drag your courage together. I don't want you acting like a coward and shaming me and Father in front of the rest of the Vigilance Committee. You just do your part."

Robert scowled. "Or what? You'll use that stick on me next?"

"If I were Father," Daniel admitted, "I'd have taken a stick to you long ago. He's too lenient with you, because you're the baby of the family. I'd have thrashed you for even *thinking* about marrying Sarah Havens, let alone *asking* his permission to wed her!"

"There's nothing wrong with Sarah! And I won't hear you speaking against her!"

"That whole family is a nest of traitors, and she's one of them. You can't wallow with the hogs and expect to stay clean."

Robert's face was burning with anger, and his fist gripped his ax handle tightly. "You have no right to say anything against her!"

"That will be enough out of the two of you!" Father's voice cut between them like a knife. Daniel's face fell back into its amiable grin, and Robert caught rein of his anger. "We're not here for you two to fight each other. Save your anger for the rebel scum."

"Of course, Father," Daniel agreed smoothly. "We were just becoming a little . . . spirited."

"Raise your spirits some other way," Father commanded, and then went back to talking in low tones with Mr. Rankine and one of the other men. They were approaching Hiram Clayton's shop now.

Robert had a bad taste in his mouth about this whole thing, but he knew he couldn't back out now. He realized that his brother was simply after causing trouble, and didn't much care who it was aimed against. His father, as always, was quite convinced of the righteousness of his own cause. But Robert had neither his father's self-assurance nor his brother's love of violence. Instead, he was filled with anxiety.

He wasn't the only one, by the look of it. Abner Marshall, one of the older men in the group, looked less than happy. This was not universally a popular move, it seemed. But nobody actually spoke up about it, and Robert knew it wasn't his place to question his elders. Besides, Father would be furious with him if he said anything. He kept silent, and tried to hold back.

Clayton's shop was actually more of a shed tacked on to the main house. Robert knew it held the printing press and supplies Hiram Clayton used to make up flyers for the town, and his small pamphlets and news sheets. There was a door directly into the shop, and one from the shop to the house, where Hiram, his wife, and their two children lived. Mr. Rankine reached the outer door and tried it. Because it was after-hours, it was bolted on the inside, and wouldn't open.

"We'd best go through the house," Father suggested. "It'll be the simplest route."

The group moved to the main door. Mr. Rankine didn't bother knocking, but instead simply flung open the door. "Come on, lads!" he called.

Robert was the last in — wishing desperately that he didn't have to go in at all, but Daniel was watching him closely. Mr. Clayton and his wife were huddled with the two young children in the kitchen, by the fire. It was dying down, ready to be banked for the night, and only one candle lit the room. The shadows thrown made the place look dark and dismal.

"What do you think you're doing?" Mr. Clayton demanded, looking at them all with obvious concern. "You have no right to come in here and scare my family!"

"And you have no right to print seditious lies and encourage treason," Mr. Rankine answered. "But you do it anyway."

"There are a great many people in these parts

who agree with what I do," the printer said defiantly.

"And a great many more who agree with what we are about to do," Robert's father growled. "You have a choice, Clayton: Either stop your treasonous actions of your own free will, or else we shall stop them for you."

"You have no right," Clayton protested again.

"We have all the right we need," Mr. Rankine answered him. He hefted his walking stick. "We have the right of any loyal subject to defend the Crown and the laws of this land. Perhaps the constables won't take action against you, rebel, but there are plenty of good and true men who will." He turned to the Vigilance Committee. "Into the shop, boys!"

One of the men carried a lantern, and with this held high, the group surged into the small, crowded room that held the press. In the uncertain light, Robert could see that there was a stack of pamphlets all finished, awaiting distribution. Mr. Rankine snatched up the top one.

"Look at this!" he cried out. "It's a reprint of a speech by that troublemaker, John Adams of Boston. *This* is what our printer has been hiding!"

"Adams is a man of sense," Mr. Clayton objected. "Everyone has a right to read what he says."

"Nobody has the right to be offended by a traitor!" Robert's father objected. Taking a spill from his pocket, he held it to the lantern. Then he turned to the pile of papers with the naked light.

"No!" the printer yelled, surging forward. He didn't get far; two of the committee grabbed his arms and pinned them back, holding him firmly as Mr. Allison torched the pamphlets. This cast a satanic light across the room; Robert felt sick. Was this the way to persuade someone of the wrongness of their deeds?

"It's not enough," Mr. Rankine decided. He looked around the room. "He'll just reprint more tomorrow, I'm sure. Let's make certain that he can't."

Daniel laughed, and jumped at the cases of type. The small lead lumps went flying as he smashed their boxes. The letters clattered across the floor, spilling in all directions. Two of the other men swung their staves at the press itself. It was too big and heavy to suffer much damage, but the handle was broken off. Another of the men grabbed one of the tubs of printer's ink and broke open its side.

Thick, black ink oozed out, soaking the floor and anything on it.

Mr. Clayton struggled to free himself and stop the vandalism. "You can't do this!" he yelled. "I'll have the law onto you!"

"The law *you* deny has any right in our country?" Mr. Allison demanded angrily. "The law *you* urge us to overthrow? Ha!" Abruptly, his fist whipped out, and he punched the printer hard across the face, drawing blood and a groan of pain. "If you don't like English law, man, then you must suffer outside of its protection." He punched the man again, a cruel blow to the stomach. Mr. Clayton could neither fight back nor escape, held firmly as he was.

"Perhaps now," Mr. Rankine thundered, "you can see the reason for law and justice? The very things that you refuse to believe in would have been your protection, had you remained a true and loyal man. But now they will do nothing for you. You have turned your back on the natural order of this world, and so you deserve all that comes to you."

"Please," a thin voice called from the doorway. It was the printer's wife. There was no sign of the children. "Leave us alone, I beg you."

"You *are* alone," Mr. Rankine replied. "You have

chosen to take yourselves out of society, and so society agrees with your own decision by expelling you. Taste the fruits of your rebellious nature."

Father punched Mr. Clayton one more time, then gestured to the men holding him up. They threw him to the floor, where he lay, battered and bleeding. One of the men then kicked him in the ribs. Mr. Clayton rolled, groaning, holding his side. His wife fell across him to protect him from any further blows.

Mr. Rankine moved forward, and stood over the poor woman. "Let us hope that this has shown you both the error of your ways," he said coldly. "Learn your lesson well, and don't fall back into sin and treason. If you do, the next time we come, we shall not burn down papers and overturn barrels. We shall burn down the house — with you all in it. If you care at all for those children of yours, remember this, and think on it." He glanced around the room. The papers were almost ashes now, and the ink had stopped spreading. Daniel had scattered all of the type and broken frames. It was a terrible mess, and everyone but Robert seemed pleased to see it. "Come along, lads," Mr. Rankine said cheerfully. "I think this has been a good evening's work. And a lesson that some people will understand had best be taken to heart." He stepped over the prone bodies on the floor and then kicked open the door to the outside.

One by one, the Vigilance Committee filed past the stunned and terrified couple. Robert's father actually spat on them. Robert was almost too ashamed of what had been done to even look at Mr. Clayton, but he forced himself to do it. The printer's eyes were both swollen, and there was a gash down his left cheek that bled onto his shirt. He was breathing hard and whimpering slightly. His wife's eyes were large with fear, and she clutched her husband convulsively.

Robert wished he could say something to apologize, to tell them that he had not wanted to be here, that he did not think what was done was right. But there were no words that came to his tongue. Instead, he stumbled from the house after the others, bitterly ashamed.

He was alone in that feeling. The other men were laughing and pounding one another on the back, as though they had won some great victory, instead of having terrorized a helpless family. Robert hung his head, hoping that nobody would talk to him, or joke with him. Or, worse, ask why he had simply stood by and done nothing. He could not tell these people the truth, that he hated what had been done. They would not understand, and would not like to hear such comments. He wanted only to get home to bed and hide his shame in the darkness.

Naturally, he didn't get his wish. Instead, his father fell in beside his heavy steps. "I am glad that you were with us tonight," he said proudly. "I had begun to wonder about you, Robert. You seem so often to be too weak to be my son. But by standing with us, you have shown me that you can be trusted." He clearly hadn't seen the sickened expression on Robert's face, and Robert had no intention of explaining his true feelings.

"As a result," Father added, "I've been rethinking my stance on your request of last night. I know my initial reaction was to reject out of hand the idea of you wedding that Havens girl. But I now think I may have been too hasty."

Robert blinked, his heart surging. He could hardly believe what he was hearing. Father admitting he might have been wrong? Better yet, holding out some hope for Robert?

"I have decided that I will give my blessing after all to your marriage." He held up a hand to cut off Robert's babbled thanks. "There is, however, a condition to this approval. One that, if you are correct about the girl, you should have no problem with."

Robert's heart sank again. This was just like Father — hold out hope, but impose impossible conditions of ever qualifying for that end. He had no idea what it was that Father wanted of him, but he knew it would be harsh. Father always believed that life was harsh, and to meet reality one had to be strong. But Robert was resolved to one thing: He would do whatever it took to win Sarah. "I'll do whatever I need to win her," he vowed.

Father looked at him with a peculiar gleam in his eye. "Oh, the condition isn't for you, my boy. It's for her."

For *Sarah*? Robert stared at his father in shock. What could his father possibly demand of Sarah?

And would she be willing to do it?

Chapter Thirteen

Joshua was roused from his sleep by violent shaking. He managed to open his eyes and stare at the worried face of Betsy, who was holding a lantern. Beyond her, the darkness was deep. Joshua could hear the snufflings of the horses, disturbed by this nighttime intruder. The straw beneath his blanket crackled as he managed to sit up. "What is it?" he asked, anxiously.

"Everyone is being roused," the serving girl answered. "There's been a messenger from Boston — the British are on the march!"

Throwing off the last traces of sleep, Joshua scrambled to his feet. "They're on their way here?"

"Yes," Betsy confirmed. "Colonel Barrett has called for everyone to assemble."

"I'm coming," he promised her. He paused only long enough in the stable to splash some water on his face to help him waken, and then followed her to the tavern. The place was once again a frenzy of movement, as the colonel barked out orders, dispatching people all over the town. Joshua pressed forward, fighting against the stream of departing men.

"What can I do to help, Colonel?" he asked. He had his musket and his powder bag with him.

Colonel Barrett looked at him grimly. "This may indeed come to a fight," he said. "But it's our fight, lad, not yours. Hold yourself ready to carry messages, and stay close by me. This is going to be a long day." He glanced back at his ledger book. "Now, excuse me — I've a great deal of supplies to hide from the British. It's obvious that they're on their way here to seize them." He turned back to giving orders again.

Betsy tapped his arm and handed him a mug of cider, which he accepted gratefully. Before she moved on, she gestured to a tired-looking man in the corner of the room. "If you want to know what's happening, go and talk to Doctor Prescott."

Joshua nodded. Sipping the cider gratefully, he went to the man and introduced himself. "Do you know what is happening?" he asked.

"As much as anyone here," the doctor replied.

"The British have made their move, leaving Boston under the cover of darkness. I was on my way back home to Lexington when I came across the silversmith, Paul Revere, and the tanner, William Dawes. They told me the news that the British were marching, and I decided to help them spread the word. They had warned Lexington, and alerted John Hancock and Samuel Adams to flee. They were on their way here next, and so I decided to turn around and aid them.

"But the British were not as lazy as we had imagined, and a mounted patrol of their officers caught us. They wanted to know where we were bound and why. I whispered to Revere, 'Put on!' and we broke for it." He shivered. "Then we ran. He was to head back for Lexington to tell Adams and Hancock that the British were already near. I rode here to alert Colonel Barrett."

Joshua felt a thrill at the thought of what the other man had been through. "Did they fire at you?"

"Aye, but it was dark, and I'm pretty lively when I must be." He smiled. "They didn't hit me, and didn't dare follow. They're after our supplies, but they don't know how many men strong we are. They're obviously waiting for their main force, which is not so far behind us now."

So the confrontation everyone had been expecting was coming! Joshua's excitement rose as he watched the minutemen receiving their instructions and rushing to obey. Despite the number of people present, it was not chaos. The mood seemed to have gripped everyone — a mix of excitement, apprehension, and adventure.

"Right!" Barrett called eventually. "I want the minutemen and the two companies of militia to assemble on the green in front of this tavern. I've sent a rider to Lexington to find out what is happening there. When he returns, we'll make our final plans. Come along, look sharp!"

Joshua, having no specific task to perform, hastily finished his cider, nodded to Dr. Prescott, and followed Colonel Barrett as he strode from the tavern.

It was still before dawn, and there was a slight chill in the April air. The town, however, was wide awake, and the fighting men were starting to filter through the streets and buildings to congregate on the green. Joshua felt proud to be with them, and worried about what might happen. The British would probably be aiming to arrest any ringleaders that they could find, which meant the colonel was in danger of landing in a British jail. But Joshua could hear the courage in the voices of the assembling men, and knew that they would never let the British take captives without a serious fight — one he hoped the British troops would not want. After the last fighting in Boston, the authorities were wary of creating fresh friction.

Light was breaking when a fresh body of men came marching into town. Joshua could see they were another bunch of minutemen. "From Lincoln," one of the men near him said. "I recognize several familiar faces there." Lincoln was a nearby town, and Joshua felt encouraged. There were over six thousand minutemen or militia in the surrounding towns; obviously, many were on their way to help out here. Concord men would not fight alone, if it came to a struggle. Joshua edged closer to the colonel, and listened in.

"There's been shooting over at Lexington," the commander of the new arrivals reported. "We heard shots as we left. The British are forcing their way, it seems."

"Shooting?" Barrett shook his head. "I can scarcely believe they'd start such trouble."

At that moment, a rider came hurtling up to the green and leaped from his horse. "Colonel!" he gasped. "The British are at Lexington, and they've fired on the men there!"

"Were they firing ball?" Barrett demanded, sounding astonished. Joshua knew he'd believed the British had to be under orders not to do so.

"I don't know," the scout admitted. "But I think it probable."

Barrett nodded and dismissed the man. Joshua had caught the rider's horse, which was sweating from the run. "I'll make sure the horse is stabled," Joshua offered. "The British really are fighting?"

"Aye," the man answered wearily. "Pitcairn and his men rode in, looking for trouble. They ordered the militia, under Captain Parker, to lay down their weapons. I rode back here, and as I left, I saw the British firing at our boys. It certainly didn't seem like it was only powder they were firing. I wish I knew what was happening there now, but it seemed more important to bring word back to the colonel than to stand and gawk."

Joshua admired the bravery of the man. He hurried the steed to one of the stable hands, with instructions to care for it, and then dashed back to where the colonel was issuing a stream of orders to his men. "We need to retain control of the road into town," he declared. "I need most of the troops on the ridge overlooking the road. Gentlemen, you will take the men there. With music! I want the

British to hear the sound of our fifes and drums! Let them know we are not afraid of them and are ready to give them all the welcome they deserve." He continued to fire off orders, deciding to send a small detachment of men down the road toward Lexington. "If they know we are ready and willing to fight, they may back down," he explained. "But I don't want to be the one to open hostilities here. If the British don't back down, I want a good, orderly retreat up to the ridge. But a loud and lively one."

The men gave a cheer, and hurried to do as the colonel had instructed. Joshua wished that he had a task, but knew he could help best by staying out of this. These men knew one another and had trained and drilled together. He would merely be in the way if he tried to join in now. Besides, the colonel might need another messenger at any moment, and he aimed to be ready if that was the case.

Another man came hurrying over, a young person in the clothing of a pastor. "Colonel!" he called as he arrived, almost breathlessly. "I see that you're in good shape. Going to attack the British in force!"

"I am not attacking, Mister Emerson," Colonel Barrett replied. "I am merely seeing to it that the

British will not receive a quiet reception when they arrive."

"Not attacking?" The minister looked shocked. "But surely you must. I have heard that the enemy has fired on our brave boys in Lexington! You must repay the British for this!"

"Mr. Emerson," the colonel said patiently enough, "the British have over a thousand troops in the field. We have a few companies, and are badly outnumbered. There are riders alerting the country-side, and we will be receiving help in a matter of hours. I would be an extremely foolish man to at-tack a larger body of men with a smaller one, espe-cially when we shall undoubtedly outnumber them in a matter of hours simply by waiting."

"But — but who knows what the British will do when they arrive?"

"I am sure we shall find out soon enough," Bar-rett suggested dryly. "In the meantime, I have work to do. Good day, sir."

"I must protest!" Mr. Emerson exclaimed. "It is your duty to attack!"

"It is not my duty to be a damned fool," the colonel growled. "I'll leave that task to you. Good day, again." He strode off, heading for his horse.

Joshua, grinning to himself at the pastor's shocked expression, followed after. He could understand the colonel's reasoning perfectly, even if the man of God could not.

It certainly looked as though there was going to be action enough. If the British were firing musket balls, then they were no longer concerned merely with keeping order; they were firmly on the attack. And there could only be one response from the patriots toward an enemy force firing upon them: They must fight back. Joshua clutched at his musket, certain he would use it this day.

He followed the colonel to the ridge, overlooking the road from Lexington. The colonel was following sound, martial strategy: He would take and keep the high ground, forcing his enemies to attack uphill. Especially given the fewer number of patriots, this was a good move. Joshua's respect for Colonel Barrett was growing the more he saw of his orders. Not everyone was as happy, though. There were plenty of grumbles that they should be out hunting the British like wild turkeys and shooting them down when they were found. The colonel ignored all such comments as if they had not been made.

There were plenty of men here, young and old.

There were some a good ten years older than the colonel, their antique muskets primed and ready for the day. They had expressions on their faces that were almost resigned, as if they had known this day was long in coming, and they had been afraid they would die before it arrived. There were boys even younger than Thomas — some barely into their teens, by the looks of them — with borrowed guns and faces that showed either excitement or fear. But not a face showed any intent of backing down a single step.

There were women, too, hurrying about. Some were helping to hide the militia's stores in cellars, attic spaces, or even in the church. Others were bringing packages of food to the men, or a jacket, or a drink. Some looked worried and nervous for their husbands and sons, but all looked ferociously determined to do what must be done. Joshua's feelings for these New Englanders swelled with pride. The British would know that they had stepped on a snake when it bit them hard this day!

There was a murmur of excitement in those waiting as they heard the sound of fifes and drums from the Concord road. The small force Colonel Barrett had sent to try and intimidate the English was returning, but in good humor and keeping a lively tune playing. At almost the same moment, Joshua caught his first glimpse of the red jackets off through the trees and down by the road.

"Steady, men," Colonel Barrett called out. "The English are coming. And if it's war they want, I'll wager they'll find plenty a man up here willing to give them what they seek."

There was a general chorus of approval at that. Joshua carefully loaded the powder into his musket and rammed home a ball. When the fighting began, he'd be ready and able to do his part.

The British were coming. . . .

Chapter Fourteen

*S*arah spent the whole night tossing and turning in her bed. She would drift in and out of sleep, and wake up shaking. Why had Robert not come?

At least the twins in the other bed were quiet for once, and didn't complain about her restlessness.

She got up earlier than usual and dressed hastily. She started the water boiling for breakfast, not because she wanted to work, but simply because doing things helped to numb her mind. Mother was pleasantly surprised when she arose and started the breakfast cooking. Thomas was up and shot off to milk the cows before the food was ready. If he was surprised to see Sarah working this early, he didn't say anything.

The twins, however, simply couldn't resist.

"Maybe Sarah in love is a good thing," Ben commented.

"Yes," Hannah agreed, grinning widely. "It makes her get up early. Hoping to see Robert today?"

"Mind your own business," Sarah snapped. She didn't know whether she wanted to see him or not, but she wasn't going to tell the twins anything. She got the salt bowl out and slammed it down on the table, almost spilling the precious commodity. Mother glared at her for this, but didn't say anything. Typical! Mother didn't understand, as usual. Couldn't she see the agony that Sarah was in? Obviously not.

Some days Sarah really hated her family.

After breakfast, she helped to do the cleaning up, and then started her household chores. Almost an hour later, there was the clatter of a horse arriving. Could it be Robert? Excitedly, fearfully, she hurried to answer the rap on the door. To her disappointment and relief, it was only the rector, Mr. Hayes. Sarah greeted him and took him into the kitchen, where Mother was in the middle of baking bread. Sarah immediately put a pot on to boil for tea.

"I really cannot stay," the rector informed them. "I am here simply as the bearer of bad news."

Sarah's heart almost stopped. Had something terrible happened to Robert? Was that why he hadn't come? Was he lying somewhere, injured or even dead? What would she do if he was?

"Last night," Mr. Hayes explained, "some men entered the house of Hiram Clayton. They beat him severely, and damaged his printing press."

"That's terrible," Mother exclaimed. "Does he know who the men were?"

"I am sure he does," the rector replied. "But he will not name them. I believe he fears that if he does they will return and do further damage. There is little doubt of the reason for the attack, though. The men burned copies of a speech of John Adams. The men clearly must have been loyalists to the Crown, upset with Mister Clayton's stance."

"That sounds quite likely," Mother agreed. "Please pass along my sympathies to the family, and tell them that if there is anything I or my family can do, they shouldn't hesitate to ask."

"I'm sure they will appreciate that," the rector said approvingly. "Meanwhile, I suggest that you keep an eye out for any people coming here in the evening."

Mother looked shocked. "You think they may come here?"

"I did not think any in our community, of whatever allegiance, would attack one of their neighbors in their home," Mr. Hayes replied. "If they have done so once, I fear it may embolden them to repeat their terrible actions. I am thus warning all the families I feel may be in their bad graces."

"It's true that I've made little secret of my own sympathy for the rebel cause," Mother agreed. "Thank you for the advice, Pastor. I promise I shall be extra careful when darkness descends." She paused. "I have to admit that I did not know that you were on our side."

"I am on neither side," Mr. Hayes said grimly. "I am a man who serves God, not a crown or a republic. But I cannot condone anyone who strikes at his neighbor by night. That is not the Christian way, and I promise I shall speak severely against it in my next sermon." He nodded to Sarah and her mother. "Good day, ladies. I have more calls to make, so I trust you will excuse me."

"Such a terrible thing to do," Mother muttered after the pastor left. "How could anyone do that to poor Mister Clayton?"

"Men can do many terrible things," Sarah said, thinking of how Robert had betrayed her.

"Especially when they feel they are in the right,"

Mother said, agreeing with her for once. Sarah was amazed. Perhaps Robert *did* feel that way!

"Do you think that Robert would be so mean?" she asked.

Mother looked puzzled. "Robert? What has he to do with the beating of Mister Clayton?"

"I was referring to his disappointing me last night," Sarah said, confused. What was wrong with Mother? Couldn't she follow a simple conversation anymore?

Mother frowned. "So the whole world still revolves about you and your emotions, does it? Do you feel no sympathy for Mister Clayton and his family?"

What did this have to do with anything? "Mister Clayton brought it upon himself," Sarah answered. "Meddling in politics always causes trouble. He should have stayed out of it."

"Politics," Mother said coldly, "is the framework for our lives. You can no more stay out of it than you can stop breathing and still expect to live. We are involved here in the struggle for our future — freedom or slavery. Nobody with a conscience can stay out of it."

"I want my future to be with Robert," Sarah protested. "That's all that concerns me."

"Yes," Mother agreed. "I can see that it is. It is such a shame that this consumes you so, but I suppose at your age and with your addled wits, I should expect no less. And if Robert is all that concerns you, then you'd better wipe that flour from your nose, because he's almost here, at the rear door."

Sarah's heart leaped in her chest like a rabbit at the hunter's gun. "Here?" she yelped. "Why didn't you warn me?" She wiped at her nose, hoping she'd cleaned it and not smudged it worse. If only she had a bucket of water handy to check her reflection in! "Do I look fine?"

"You look as well as you ever do," Mother answered. "And I thought you were ready to thrash him about the ears for what he did to you."

"Don't be silly, Mother." Sarah bolted for the door, catching a glimpse of Robert through the window as she passed her mother. She opened the door and watched her beloved, her traitor, approaching. He looked as handsome as ever, but also strangely disturbed.

"Sarah," he said. She loved hearing him say her name.

"Robert. I missed you yesterday."

He had the grace to blush and look away. "I was . . . unavoidably detained," he stammered. "I *wanted* to come, and I tried, but my father wouldn't hear of it."

"Your father?" Sarah's heart fell again. The hunter had shot the rabbit. "He refused permission?"

Robert looked agonized. "We have to talk alone," he said. Then, with a guilty start, "Ah, Mistress Havens, if you will permit me to speak with Sarah in private?"

"I think you had better do so, before she bursts and ruins my clean floor," Mother said, making a poor joke of Sarah's distress. "Afterward perhaps you and I should also speak."

"Of course." Robert stood aside, and Sarah slipped from the house, carefully closing the door behind her. She didn't want Mother listening in on her private talk with Robert. He glanced around, and gestured off toward the vegetable garden. "Perhaps over here?"

Sarah nodded and accompanied him in silence. She wished she knew what was happening! How did Robert feel about her? What had his father said? Why all this mystery?

When would he kiss her again?

They reached the garden, and Robert simply stood there for a moment. Then he grasped her hands again. "Sarah, I'm sorry about last night. I did try to come, but . . . well, Father had things he wanted me to do. I couldn't get away. I know you must be furious with me for that — "

"Of course not!" Sarah exclaimed. "I knew there had to be a reason you weren't there. I didn't doubt you for a minute. So what did your father say about us?"

He looked uncomfortable. "Well, at first he was completely against it."

Sarah gasped as if she had been struck. "He *refused* you?" It was what she had been dreading and fearing. The worst possible thing had happened!

"Only at first," Robert said hastily. "Then he changed his mind and gave his approval."

"He did?" Sarah wanted to scream and jump for joy, but that would be undignified for a woman about to be wed. "Oh, Robert, that is wonderful! When can we marry, then? Soon, I pray!"

Again, he looked a little uncomfortable. "He did make his permission contingent upon one condition," he added.

"A condition?" Who cares? She shrugged. "Anything, so that we can be together." She pressed his hands to her heart, and he blushed. "Oh, Robert, I am so glad. We are to be wed."

"The condition," he reminded her. Stopping her own burbling, she nodded. "As you know," Robert said, "my father is a staunch loyalist. He believes that the king is our God-appointed ruler, and I agree with him."

Sarah shrugged. "What does that matter?" she asked, puzzled. "It matters little to me who rules our land, as long as we can be together."

"It matters much to my father," Robert explained. "He agrees to our marriage only on the stipulation that you publicly announce that you, too, support the loyalist cause. He will not allow me to wed anyone who is not a supporter of the king."

"Is that all?" Sarah asked, almost laughing with relief. "Robert, as I said, I don't care *who* rules in the Colonies. All I care about is us. I'd swear allegiance to the heathen Turks if that is what it takes for us to be together."

Robert looked immensely relieved. "Then you have no problem with this condition?"

"Of course not." Sarah shook her head. "It's completely unimportant to me. Of course I'll swear to be loyal to the king, if that is what it takes."

"Oh, Sarah," Robert breathed. "I knew you'd feel that way. I knew you were on the right side, and wouldn't stand with your family."

"My family?" Sarah was confused again. "What do they have to do with it?"

Robert blinked. "Well, they are, of course, in favor of rebellion."

She shrugged. "As I said, that has nothing to do with us. Let them all have their politics. All I want is you."

"But . . ." He looked bewildered. "Surely you understand what is going to happen?"

"We are going to be married," Sarah said patiently. What was wrong with him?

"Sarah," he said gently, "if you swear allegiance to the king, then you must also denounce your family as traitors. You must cut yourself off from them."

She was absolutely stunned. What was he talking about? "I don't understand," she confessed, scared. "Why must I do that?"

"You have to show that you don't secretly harbor the same wrong beliefs as your family," he explained. "You must disavow them in public. And they are bound to cast you out for it."

Sarah was in shock. "Denounce them?" she muttered, her head in a whirl. "Cast out?" She looked sharply at him. "They would never do that to me."

"They would have no choice," he said gently. "If

you say in public that they are traitors, they can do nothing else but cast you out."

"Traitors?" This was all too much for Sarah. "But this is all politics!" she cried. "It has *nothing* to do with us!"

"It has *everything* to do with us," Robert corrected her. "Our families stand opposed to one another at this moment. You have to choose which side you will be on. If you truly want to marry me, then the choice is surely simple. If you agree to the condition, my father will approve our marriage and give us land for a farm of our own. We can start our lives together."

"But . . ." Sarah didn't know what to think. "My mother would never agree to marriage under those conditions. She is very stubborn; I know her."

"Father will speak to the town council," Robert promised. "He has influence, and they will grant us a license, even without your mother's approval. They are in the majority loyal to the Crown, and know where your mother's loyalties lie. We can do it without her."

Without Mother? Sarah stood there, pulled in two different directions. It would be so simple to follow her heart, to marry Robert and to have the life she had dreamed of.

But to do so, she would lose her family. . . .

The twins — annoying brats . . . putting toads in her bed, hiding her clothes. Teasing her and mocking her. Poking their noses into her business and spying on her private moments.

Thomas — so sure of his own causes, sneering so at her wishes and dreams. Calling her bossy and complaining about her constantly.

Joshua — well, he wasn't so bad, really. He called her lazy, but he did little else.

Mother — never understanding her, always ignoring her feelings. Trying to make Sarah sound like she was a shallow idiot just because she had simple dreams.

And, on the other side, Robert! Tall and strong and gentle. Caring, compassionate. Someone who would love her and never think ill of her.

Would it be so hard to give up her family for that?

And yet . . .

Yes, the twins were annoying. But they could also be loving. And sometimes they were funny. Could she live without their laughter? And Thomas acted so superior, but he also helped her with her chores if she was a little behind, and he looked after her when he could. Joshua treated her like a lady. And Mother — well, for all of her faults, Sarah never doubted for an instant that her mother loved her. She might often be wrong, but her decisions were always made for Sarah's good — even if her idea of what was good for Sarah wasn't correct.

Could she give that up, even for Robert? She didn't know.

But perhaps it wouldn't be necessary?

Filled with her idea, Sarah exclaimed, "Could we not do it the other way around?"

"I don't understand," Robert said, his face creased with confusion.

"Could you not decide to become a rebel, and join my family instead?" Sarah was almost exploding with the idea. "Mother would welcome you, I know. She thinks highly of you, you see."

"But . . ." He was at a loss for words. "That simply isn't possible. I can't go against my father's wishes."

"What?" Sarah stared at him, stunned, her idea and dreams decaying around her. "You cannot go against your father's wishes? And yet you expect *me* to deny my mother and family?"

"But . . . they are *traitors*," he said, trying to make himself understood. "They are *wrong*. I know that you are too wise to believe in their cause, and that you love me enough to . . ." His voice trailed off. "You *do* love me?" he asked, clearly disturbed.

"More, it would seem, than you love me," Sarah answered. "I, at least, considered doing as you demanded. I would gladly swear my loyalty to a king I do not believe in. Yet you would not go against your father's wishes for my sake."

"It's not the same thing," Robert protested.

"It would appear not," Sarah agreed. Coldness was starting to form around her heart, like the ice on a water bucket in the winter. "I am the one who must deny her family. I am the one who must leave everyone she knows and loves. I am the one who must suffer."

"But we will be able to be married. Is that not worth it?"

Sarah couldn't help recalling how rude Mr. Allison had been to her mother at church. At the time she had been embarrassed by her mother's actions, but now she realized she was more annoyed by Mr. Allison's harsh words. "And we will live together at your father's demands, on his charity — as long as he wishes to give it? And what about further demands that he might make? Will you knuckle down to those also — whatever they cost?"

"I don't understand," Robert protested. "He is only making one condition!"

"*Now* he is making only one," Sarah answered. The ice was almost perfectly formed now. "And will he vow that he will never make another? Will he trust that, once I have made my fealty to the king, I will never change my mind again? Or will he demand some guarantees? It seems to me, Robert, that you have already made your own choice in this matter. You have chosen your family over me. How can I do any less? It seems to me that your father's condition is not so much to secure my loyalty to the king as it is to simply embarrass my family in public. Oh, I'm sure he'll be happy to be able to say, 'Here is my daughter-in-law. She has scorned her family to show the world that I am right.' He would love that!"

"I'm sure that's not what he intends," Robert said.

"Are you? Are you truly?"

He considered a moment, and then shook his head. "No," he said, almost in a whisper. "No, I am not so sure, after all."

"But I am." Sarah's heart was as cold as ice now. "I am sorry, Robert, but I cannot marry you on that condition. I will not turn my back on my family."

"Not even for our love?" he begged her.

"Not even for that." She softened slightly. "If you should ever decide that you can accept me unconditionally, then you may repeat your offer of marriage. If you cannot do that, then we have nothing more to say to each other."

Robert looked as if he had been shot through the heart. He stumbled, trying to find something to say. But nothing came out. Downcast and dejected, he turned away and slowly walked off.

Sarah watched him go, her heart completely ice. She was not affected.

As soon as he was out of sight, the ice melted, and poured from her eyes.

Chapter Fifteen

*R*obert's footsteps picked up as his thoughts and emotions changed. At first, leaving the Havens farm, he was heartbroken. He could hardly bring himself to believe that Sarah had rejected him. He had been so sure that she would see the wisdom of his father's offer and jump at the chance for them to be married. Of course, he understood that it wouldn't be easy for her to tear herself away from her mother and family to join him. Women were weak in that way. But Robert knew he was right to ask; Mrs. Havens was a troublemaker, and would only get herself and the rest of her family into serious problems with her terrible attitude. He had been so *sure* that Sarah would understand that.

So why hadn't she? There was only one possible explanation: that she really didn't love him as much as he had hoped. If she had loved him as he loved her, she would have agreed to his father's condition.

And that hurt him. He had been so certain that she was the one for him, and he had been so wrong. And, not only that, she had even had the nerve to ask that *he* give up his family instead! As if *he* were in the wrong somehow! How *could* she? Surely she must understand that the Allison family was right to be loyalists and that the Havens were wrong to be rebels?

There was only one possible explanation: Father had been right. She wasn't really in love with him; she was simply trying to subvert him, to make him defect from the right side to the wrong. Like Eve with the apple tempted Adam to sin, Sarah Havens had tried to tempt him into it.

No wonder Father had never married again! Women were all like Sarah and Mrs. Robson — scheming, manipulative little witches, trying to lure a man into doing what was wrong. Robert realized he was well rid of her.

But he *missed* her so. . . . His footsteps became leaden again as he pictured Sarah's smiling face, radiant with her inner joy, or proud and firm with her convictions. She was the prettiest girl he knew, as well as the smartest. How could he live without her?

And that was what she was counting on, wasn't it? That he would think of her eyes, her smile, her pretty ankles — and that wonderful, wonderful kiss. But he would show her! He wasn't going to think about them! He wasn't going to fall into the oldest trap known to man. He wouldn't be lured astray by the wiles of a woman!

Walking faster, he felt the anger growing within his heart. She turned him down, insulted him and his family, and tried to seduce him into evil. What a heartless, cold, scheming person! And to think he had almost fallen into her trap! It was so humiliating. Daniel was right, he should set his sights on a *sensible* girl. Maybe he wouldn't end up with the most beautiful, brightest, or most fun. But he would get a *nice* girl. Not Sarah Havens.

But it was Sarah that he wanted. . . .

His heart ached, and he couldn't take his mind off her. He didn't know whether he loved her or hated her; he did know that he was obsessed by her. He had to do something. He had to forget her somehow, drive her from his mind. There had to be other girls whose lips were just as kissable, whose eyes were so bright, whose personality sparkled.

He couldn't think of any other one.

Abruptly, Daniel was there, leaning on a fence post and grinning at him. "What's wrong?" he asked, stirring slightly. "Didn't your sweetheart want to play house?"

"She turned me down," Robert said, humiliated and angry.

"Well, what did you expect?" His brother moved to join him, putting a friendly arm about his shoulders. "Did you *really* think she was any different from the rest of her family? Robert, you were so naive to think she'd come to her senses and join our family."

"I guess I was," Robert admitted, miserably. "But . . . I was so *sure*."

"Girls can do that to you." Daniel grinned again. "They affect your senses, if you let them. They weasel their ways into your emotions and play on them. Did she let you kiss her?"

Robert flamed with embarrassment. "Of course not! She's not that kind of girl!" He squirmed. "Well," he added, compelled by honesty, "she did let me kiss her on the lips."

"There you go," Daniel said with conviction. "The same lips that lied to you, right? She was trying to poison you against us, wasn't she?" He shook his head. "You don't have to say anything; I can read it on your face, as plain as flies on cow pats."

"She *did* try to make me go over to the revolutionary cause," Robert admitted, ashamed to say it.

"I *told* you she was as bad as the rest of them. You can't expect anything better from her. And you were too smart to do that, I can see. Father would have cut you off without a penny if you had done anything so foolish. And you can't live without money."

"That's not why I turned her down," Robert protested. "It was because I *know* we're fighting on the side of right. These rebels are troublemakers and malcontents. How could I join them and be true to myself?"

Daniel shrugged. "Well, that's a good reason, too. But it doesn't hurt to recall who has the money here; the Havenses are nearly paupers, and Father is quite wealthy. When the time comes, he'll settle a good amount on the both of us — as long as we agree with him in all things."

Robert looked at his brother, wondering. Was Daniel mouthing his respect for Father simply in the hopes of inheriting money? Surely that couldn't be what he was saying?

"Anyway," Daniel continued, "it's clear that you

need to forget her. I'll help you to find one twice as handsome as Sarah Havens, and with a right-thinking mind to better her. You've got my word on that."

"Thank you, Daniel," Robert said. He was almost grateful for the offer. "But I don't think I want anything to do with girls again for a while."

"A broken heart, eh?" Daniel laughed. "Well, it'll mend soon enough. And I think I have just the medicine to cure it."

"Not another girl," Robert begged. Any girl right now would look vastly inferior to Sarah, he knew.

"Better than a girl," Robert promised. "Mister Rankine has come over. He and Father are preparing for our next lesson from the Vigilance Committee."

Robert's first reaction was to say something strong against the committee. He still hadn't forgotten what they had done the other night. But images of the betrayer, Sarah, blotted out his anger about that. Maybe doing something for the community was what he needed to enable him to forget about Sarah. "We're going to strike again?"

"We are indeed," Daniel promised. "Tomorrow night."

"Against whom?"

"I don't know yet," Daniel admitted. "Father and Mister Rankine are discussing it alone. But Father asked me to bring you to him as soon as you returned, so I'm sure they'll let us know then."

Robert knew what he needed now was a lesson to remind himself why he was a loyalist. Showing some dumb rebel the error of his ways should do that quite nicely. It would also show Sarah that he couldn't be tempted away from the path that was right. She should have *known* he would never forsake the king's cause.

They had reached the house, and entered through the kitchen door. Mrs. Robson was there, overseeing the making of dinner. She sniffed when she saw them.

"Back from your courting?" she asked, a sneer in her voice. "And what did the young woman say?"

"Turned him down flat," Daniel said cheerfully. "Well, she's a foolish one, that's for sure. Refusing to a step up in the world!"

"Only to be expected from a person in *that* family," Mrs. Robson sniffed.

Daniel led Robert into the parlor. Father and Mr. Rankine looked up from their tea and discussion. British tea, of course, with the revenues all paid to show their loyalty.

"Need I ask how it went?" Father said, almost purring. "From the look on your face, she turned you down, boy."

"She did," Robert agreed. He felt sick and disconsolate. "I was wrong about her, Father. She's as bad as the rest of her family. She even asked me to go over to the rebel cause."

"Well, I'm proud to see that you've more sense and loyalty than to do such a thing," his father replied. "You're an Allison, boy, even if you can be distracted by earthly temptations and the wiles of a pretty face."

"It won't happen again," Robert vowed, his cheeks burning. "I've learned my lesson, Father."

"I believe that you have." Father turned to Mr. Rankine. "And I think we have just the way to make certain that this truth is driven home to all concerned."

Puzzled, Robert asked, "What do you mean?"

"I mean that the next target for our Vigilance Committee has been decided upon," Father informed him. "Tonight, we visit the Havens farm and get them to stop their rebellious ways."

"The Havenses?" Robert echoed. He didn't know what to think.

But Daniel did. Laughing, he clapped Robert on

the back. "The perfect answer!" he exclaimed. "We shall show them all what their evil ways will bring down on their heads. And it will free Robert from their spell forever. Think, brother: You will be able to break free from that girl's enticements. Show her who is right and who is wrong. And show her how foolish she was to scorn your love."

Robert thought about it for a moment and then nodded. Daniel was right: He *would* show Sarah how foolish she had been to refuse his offer. She and her whole family had to understand that they were in the wrong.

Maybe it would even show Sarah the pathway back to righteousness. Maybe he could still get her to agree to marry him!

"Yes," he agreed. "Yes. I think that is a wonderful idea. We shall show them. We shall show them all."

Chapter Sixteen

Joshua remained close to Colonel Barrett as the leader of Concord's militia watched from the ridge as the British troops approached the town. There seemed to be so many of them, and so few Colonists to meet them.

"Aren't we going to attack?" one of the men grumbled.

"No," the colonel decided. He had been receiving messages all the while. "The ammunition and powder has been well hidden, so there's nothing for the British to claim. I see no need at this moment to engage them in action."

That caused a few muttered comments, but no outright rebellion. It wasn't a popular decision, but Joshua knew it was a wise one. They had control of the heights, and the British couldn't possibly achieve their objectives. If they waited, the reinforcements would arrive to help the rebels. It was a longer path for the British to get extra troops in, and there would be plenty of warning of their approach.

As they watched, Joshua could see that the British forces were now splitting up. They had reached the town, and some troops were sent to the South Bridge over the Concord River. More were sent to the North Bridge, and then a bunch of the grenadiers were sent through the town itself. Pitcairn, it seemed, was determined to find the supplies. Well, good luck to him! Joshua doubted he'd find anything; these Concord folks seemed to be well organized and knew what to do.

It was around eight in the morning now, the day quite bright and clear. Men were arriving, but Joshua could see that there were no more than a few hundred of them still. Many were muttering under their breath as the British moved unopposed through the town. They wanted badly to fight, no matter how unwise it might be.

"Look!" one man exclaimed, pointing. In the still, early morning air, smoke was rising from the center of the town. Joshua couldn't make out what was being burned, but it caused concern among the men. Samuel, who was now next to Joshua, nudged his arm and pointed at a man who was just arriving.

"Joseph Hosmer," Samuel muttered. "He and the colonel don't get along well. We may see more sparks here than the British are raising below."

Hosmer glared at Barrett, who looked mildly back at him. "The British are in our town," Hosmer stated in a voice loud enough for many to hear. "They are boasting that they could burn every town and village in the Colony and we would not stop them." He gestured dramatically at the smoke below. "Are you going to let them burn down the town?"

It was mostly theatrics, Joshua knew, but it was effective. The men had already been surly about not attacking the British before; the thought that the enemy was burning down their homes was too much to take. Barrett, no fool, could see that he was losing the support of his men, and that would be a dangerous event. Without firm leadership, the minutemen and militia would be a sorry army and stand no chance against the disciplined Englishmen.

"All right," the colonel decided. "I am not sure that they are burning the town. It's probably no more than a bonfire of what they managed to discover. But we shall go down and see what they are up to, and set everyone's minds at rest. Prepare to move out." He glanced around. "Captain Davis, are you willing to lead the march?"

The man addressed nodded eagerly. "I haven't a man that's afraid to go," he vowed.

As they prepared to move out, Barrett sighed. "I pray that this is not a mistake," he muttered. "We are giving up the height here."

Joshua followed his gaze. There were a number of English troops beside the North Bridge, ready and waiting — at least a hundred, Joshua figured. "Will they block us, Colonel?" he asked.

"I don't think so," Barrett answered. "What would be the point? They have no orders to fire first, I am sure, and I do not intend to start any fighting myself if it can be avoided. They cannot block us from going to our homes without good reason, and they have none so far."

"They may take our muskets and rifles as a reason," Joshua pointed out.

"We are entitled to raise a militia and to practice," Barrett answered with a grin.

The men started to move out, heading down the slope toward the bridge. As they passed in twos, Colonel Barrett called out, "Remember, lads: Don't shoot first." Joshua hoped that the men were paying attention. He wished he was going down with them, but his place was beside the colonel, ready to carry any needed messages. He could see what was happening clearly, though.

The British seemed amazed. One of the fifers with the militia had struck up a lively tune for them to march to. At the bridge, the British troops pulled back, crossing to the far side, and forming up a reception party, rifles at the ready. If they expected this to intimidate the Americans, it didn't work. There was much shouting of insults and jeering.

Then a couple of the British officers ran onto the bridge. They started to pry at the planks, tearing one free. Joshua frowned, realizing their aim: They could stop the march without firing a shot.

"Here!" one of the militia members yelled out. "Stop that this instant!" The men with him raised their weapons. Obviously afraid, the British officers retreated again, leaving the bridge substantially intact. The British troops now raised their rifles and fired a volley. Joshua's heart leaped, but he saw that it had been a warning only, and the rifles had been discharged into the river.

The militia scorned to stop at this warning. On they marched, reaching the edge of their side of the bridge. Joshua stared down, his nerves taut and his mouth dry. It was the moment of truth.

More of the British fired, only this time directly into the local troops. The sound, even at a distance, was loud, and smoke rose from the guns. Two of the Americans fell, one being Captain Davis, the leader of the march.

"The British are firing shot," Samuel gasped. "They've killed our men!"

"Fire, fellow soldiers," one of the militiamen yelled. "For God's sake, fire!"

It was not what Colonel Barrett had wanted, but there was no stopping events now. The British had fired first, and the militia had been given no orders about defending themselves. The militia's guns spat flame and ball. Joshua felt his stomach wrench as he heard the crash of sound and smelled the tang of the burnt powder. The shots plowed into the British — ludicrously easy targets, since they all wore red jackets. The coats of the officers were brighter than poppies, making them doubly easy to pick out.

The British fired back, and then the next set of Americans was at the bridge, howling and firing. Barrett and the last of the men moved forward, the colonel's lips tight. Joshua knew the colonel was regretting this necessity, but understood he had no other course left to him.

Seeing themselves outnumbered, the British broke and ran. A number of them were unable to flee; Joshua wasn't sure whether they were dead or alive and merely wounded. He had never seen anyone killed before.

He passed the body of Captain Davis, blood still pouring from the wound that had ripped into his chest. Joshua gagged, and hurried past, onto the bridge itself. He could see by now that some of the British, including officers, were dead. The militiamen were yelling ahead of him as they pushed the running enemy back.

"Steady!" the colonel called. "Move with care. They may have broken, but there are plenty more behind who may not be so flighty."

The British were retreating toward the center of the town. A runner came up to Colonel Barrett. "They're pulling back," the youth reported, gasping for breath. "They've called all their troops together."

"We gave them more than they could take," one of the minutemen called, laughing. "It's all over before breakfast, too."

"Over?" Barrett shook his head. "It has barely begun. The shots fired this morning won't die out quite so soon."

Joshua knew what he meant. It was one thing for the British to kill people they considered to be American rioters and troublemakers. But there were British troops dead this morning, including a number of officers. The British king and Parliament would demand retribution for this.

"Steady, men, steady," Barrett called out. "I think the British have had more than they can stomach for now. Let's just wait and see what they do."

To Joshua's amazement, the men with him seemed to simply drift off. Many, expressing their hunger, went off to find breakfast where they could. It seemed astonishingly disorganized to him. If the British rallied and struck now, Colonel Barrett could be captured or even killed.

But the British didn't rally. Instead, they gathered together in the center of Concord, warily watching, their rifles ready. Someone brought food and drink to the colonel, and Joshua managed to get a little. He was surprised to discover he was quite hungry.

If this was war, it was an odd way of fighting. Colonel Barrett dispatched some of the townswomen to collect the bodies of their fallen; the British dead were left where they were. There were a number of wounded from both sides, who were taken to local houses or churches to be tended by the surgeons. Joshua watched silently as they were carried past. It brought back bitter memories of his father's death. He had been only ten, and it had hurt him badly to lose the man who meant the most to him. He could only imagine how the youngsters of Concord would feel when they discovered their own fathers had been killed.

After a couple of hours, the British began to retreat from the town, clearly aiming for Boston. As Barrett had expected, the English had found no vital supplies. They were retreating like dogs with their tails between their legs, licked and demoralized.

"They're not so invincible," Samuel commented. "We can beat them any time we like."

"It's not over yet," Barrett growled. He glanced around. "Let's get the men moving, parallel to the British. The other militias have started to group. There will be another battle shortly. We're heading for Meriam's Corner. Spread the word to move out."

So, as Joshua had feared, it was far from over.

The British had begun this, and they had already tasted retribution for their folly. He gripped his unfired musket and started off after the colonel. Beside him, Samuel shouldered his own weapon, whistling cheerfully. He was obviously looking forward to more action. But Joshua could only think about the faces of the dead, the stench of blood, and the cries of the wounded as they were moved. Whatever war was, it was not fun.

He wasn't sure his own courage would hold up. But he didn't want to fail anyone. Unlike the others, he was silent as he marched.

Chapter Seventeen

*T*homas was confused by the change in his sister Sarah. She had obviously been crying, and he knew why: She and Robert had parted this morning. He had expected this to have made her either all weepy for the rest of the day, or else angry with everyone, scolding them without end. Instead, she was quiet and polite. A little distant, perhaps, when she was thinking of Robert, but actually easier to live with than she had been for a long while.

At midday, they all stopped for a quick lunch. Mother clearly knew more than she was confessing to, but she kept her peace. Surprisingly, it was Sarah who broke the tense silence.

"I owe you an apology, Mother," she said quietly. "You were quite right."

Mother gave a faint smile. "About what in particular?"

"That politics is an inescapable part of life. We have to make our choices, and live our lives accordingly."

"Ah." Mother nodded. "Robert asked you to make a choice, then?"

"Yes." Sarah bit at her lower lip. "He asked me to go over to the loyalist cause."

"And why didn't you?" Thomas couldn't help blurting out. "You've said often enough that you've no interest in the fight for our freedom."

"Because to become a loyalist, I'd have had to denounce all of you." Sarah looked around the table; for once, the twins weren't making fun of her. "And I simply couldn't do that."

Thomas felt a peculiar tightness in his throat. Unusually, he couldn't think of anything snappy to say back to her. He glanced at Mother, and thought her eyes looked rather teary.

"I'm very glad to hear that, Sarah," she said, and patted his sister's hand. "I know it must have been hard for you, but it was the best decision in the end. I know you probably don't think that right now, but you'll come to understand it."

"Oh, I know it was the best decision," Sarah said. "But it still hurts. But the other decision would have hurt me much more in the end. I could see that."

After lunch, Sarah went out to the barn to work the butter churn. Thomas followed her, and she didn't even snap at him. Finally, he managed to say, "I'm proud of you, you know."

"Well," Sarah said, as she slopped the cream into the churn, "I don't remember you ever saying that before."

"I don't remember ever feeling it before," he confessed. "But now I do. I guess I'd better go now, huh?"

"Perhaps you should," Sarah admitted. She looked like she was about ready to start crying again. "I've got to get my work done, after all." It was just an excuse, and they both knew it. But Thomas nodded, so she could save her pride.

"Me, too," he agreed. "Without Joshua around to pull his weight, I have to be twice as busy." He turned to go, and then stopped dead in his tracks. Beside him, Sarah gave a strangled gasp.

In the doorway stood Robert Allison.

"I'm sorry," Robert said, miserably. "I didn't mean to come back and cause problems. It's just . . ."

Thomas glanced at his sister's face. She was going through so many emotions that he couldn't even begin to decide how she must feel. Why had Robert come back? To apologize? To ask her to change her mind? To change his own? "I guess I'd better leave the two of you alone," Thomas said diplomatically.

"No!" To his surprise, both Robert and Sarah said this at the same instant. Then they looked guiltily at each other. Thomas realized that neither wanted to be left alone with the other. What was going on?

"When you turned me down," Robert said to Sarah, slowly, as if each word were being ripped individually from his throat, "I was mad at first. I wanted revenge. And I was going to do it, too. It's all planned. But then . . ." He shook his head. "I don't care what you decided, I can't bring myself to really hurt you, Sarah. So I knew I had to come and warn you, no matter what you think of me."

"What are you talking about?" Thomas asked. Sarah's lips were white, pressed hard together. It was clearly all she could do to avoid crying.

"The Vigilance Committee," Robert answered. "It's coming after you tonight."

With a shock, Thomas suddenly realized what was happening. "The people who beat up Mister Clayton?" he asked. Robert nodded. "You're one of them?" Again, Robert nodded. "How could you?"

"You don't understand," Robert said, obviously in pain.

"You're right about that," Thomas agreed. "I

don't. I mean, your brother — sure. Daniel's a mean one. But you always seemed decent enough. How could you agree to do such a thing?"

"I didn't know they were going to hurt him," Robert answered, twisting his hands together in distress. "But he's a rebel, and he prints all these lies about the king, so he needed to be taught a lesson. I didn't know he was going to get hurt."

"What did you think they would do to him?" Thomas asked incredulously. "Slap his hand and tell him he was a naughty boy? Robert, you're a jackass!"

"I know." Robert hung his head miserably.

"But you came to warn us," Sarah said softly.

"I thought I wanted to hurt you for rejecting me," Robert answered. "But I can't go through with it. I *won't* go through with it."

"Good for you," Thomas decided. "But the others will?"

Robert nodded. "I thought that you could all go away tonight, or something."

Thomas sighed. "Look, we can't just leave the farm like that. If they come and we aren't here, they'll probably kill the animals and break anything they can. Maybe even set fire to the house."

"We could fetch the constable," Sarah suggested.

She was clearly starting to realize the trouble they were in.

"If they knew he was here, they'd just go away and come back another night," Thomas objected. "It wouldn't make them give up. We have to make certain that they go away and don't come back."

"How can we do that?" Sarah asked.

"I don't know yet," Thomas admitted. "But I'm the man of the house. I'll think of something. I'll ask Mother what we can do." He looked at Robert. "What about you? Are you with us or against us?"

Robert squirmed. "I can't be either," he said miserably. "I've done all I can in warning you. I shouldn't really have done that. Only . . ." He looked at Sarah. "I couldn't let them hurt you."

Straddling the fence. As always. Thomas sighed again. "One of these days, you know, you're going to have to make a stand. You have to either face off with your father or knuckle right under to him."

"I can't go against him."

"No, I suppose you can't." Thomas turned to his sister. "We'd better go and talk with Mother." He looked back at Robert. "Maybe it would be best if you left now. If Daniel finds out you were here, he'll beat you for sure, even if you are his brother."

"You're probably right." Robert looked worried.

"Good-bye, Sarah. Be well." Then he turned and hurried off.

Sarah reached out a hand and then snatched it back. "Good-bye, Robert," she whispered, and there were definitely tears on her cheeks. She sniffed and brushed them away with the back of her hand. "Well," she said, her voice cracking, "we'd better tell Mother. What *are* we going to do?"

"There's only one thing we can do," Thomas assured her, putting as much steel as he could into his voice. "We have to strike back. We have to show this Vigilance Committee that we won't be intimidated. We have to hurt them more than they hurt us, so they'll never come back."

"How will we ever do that?"

"I don't know," Thomas confessed. "I was really hoping Mother had some ideas."

"Some man of the house you are." But she said it with clear affection in her voice, and not like a complaint. Not like the old Sarah at all.

Chapter Eighteen

*J*oshua hurried along with the colonel and the other militiamen toward Meriam's Corner, a small farmstead out on the Boston Road. The British were spread out over the road and the nearer fields as they marched, trying to flush out the patriots, without much success. After all, these were local men, and they knew the area far better than the invading English. The ridge that Colonel Barrett had held earlier gradually wore down, and came to nothing at the Corner. Here, also, the road crossed the river once again. The British would have to come by here to retreat to Boston. It was a good place to stand and fight. There were plenty of low stone walls, common in the New England area, for the militia to take shelter behind.

And there were now plenty of them. Joshua wasn't certain how many, but the colonel estimated about 600 men had now arrived, having heard of the fighting, and they were ready and eager to get their own licks in at the hated British troops. It seemed as though there was a gun behind every foot of the walls. Beyond the Meriam farm, the road twisted and wound through small dips and hollows. There were fields to one side and heavy woods to the other. As Joshua looked around, he could see more and more patriots arriving by the minute.

Then the British appeared, marching and scouting. They were still arrogant, even in retreat, and looking for someone to punish. Well, they had come to the wrong place to gain a victory! The militiamen howled their defiance, and then the gunfire began again.

Powder stank and clouded the air, and projectiles from both sides whizzed out. Joshua shot off his gun, but couldn't see whether he'd hit anyone at all. A musket ball winged off the stone about a foot from his head. "Missed us!" one minuteman yelled out, laughing. But it had been close.

Abruptly, Joshua realized that there was a definite possibility here that he might be injured or killed. Most of the British shot had gone high — they were not the crack shots the Americans were — but they were starting to find their range as round after round was fired. Joshua reloaded his musket and shot again. He didn't know whether he was relieved or disappointed when he missed. Not only could he be killed or injured — he might inflict the same on another human being. True, it was the enemy, but still the enemy was a man with a family, much the same as Joshua. Could he bring himself to do that to another person?

But what choice did he have? What kind of a future would the Colonies have if they gave in to the British? How could Joshua raise a family as slaves to a foreign king who didn't care for his subjects? How could he condemn his mother and siblings to live under such a tyrant's grip?

He loaded and fired again, and then came the call to fall back. He could see the British infantrymen were charging the walls. Wisely, the militia wasn't waiting. The British were trained to fight primarily with their bayonets, which were fixed at the end of their rifles. The Americans weren't used to this style of fighting, so getting out of the way was a smart idea. Joshua stuck close to Colonel Barrett as they retreated quickly.

But not far. Some of the men went into the woods, ready to fire on the troops from there. The rest swarmed into the fields beside the river, taking

whatever cover they could. As the British continued their march, the patriots kept them under a
constant hail of fire. Several of the British troops
fell, wounded or killed. Always, the militia fell
back, and the British continued their march.

"Hardy's Hill," Barrett said, gesturing at the rise
they were approaching. There was a large bunch of
militiamen already there, grinning and waiting for
their targets to show. "Nixon's men," the colonel
said, approvingly. "As good a group of men as you'll
find anywhere."

Joshua reloaded and joined them. His musket
barrel was warm from all the firing, and the smoke
stung his eyes and throat. He was getting tired, but
there was an exhilaration to all of this, too. The
British were being shown that they couldn't trample good Americans as they wished! It was a lesson
they were learning painfully this day.

Nixon's men laid down a withering fire as the
redcoats approached. Joshua fired again, reloaded,
and fired. He could hear the screams of men, dying
and injured, and had to force himself not to feel
sorrow or sympathy. They were the enemy, after
all. . . .

He had no idea how long it continued. All he
could think about was firing. He had no idea if he

actually hit anyone. He didn't know how he would react if he saw some young English trooper go down, bleeding from a ball of his. The militia moved back as the British pressed forward again, and then the retreat road was clear. Firing constantly, the invaders moved off down the road.

"They won't get far," Barrett predicted. "The locals are coming by the score and hundreds. As soon as we're gathered together, we shall follow." It took a short while to organize the men again, and then they were off down the road, in the wake of the British.

Samuel had turned up with a bloodstained rag wrapped about his left shoulder. "You've been hurt!" Joshua exclaimed.

"Not as badly as the British have been," Samuel answered. This was true enough. The dead and wounded had been left where they had fallen. So, too, were portions of the soldiers' equipment, which were quickly snatched up by the militia as spoils.

There was the sound of further firing ahead, and Barrett looked satisfied. "The British have found the men of Lexington again, by the sound of it," he said. "And, by God, those good men have some payment to deliver." He was clearly right, because the fresh firing forced the British advance to halt again. That gave Barrett's forces the time to catch up and start firing into the British rear.

The British soldiers had clearly reached their limits. Some of the younger ones threw down their guns and knelt in the road, surrendering and pleading for mercy. Others simply fled forward, breaking ranks and sending their officers into furious screaming fits. The British retreat was turning into an utter rout. One of the British officers rode up and down, yelling commands to his men. The British marines moved to shield the main force from Barrett's men. They were brave enough and held their ground, but they took a crippling fire, with nowhere to hide from the American guns.

Joshua fired as if in a dream. People were falling, dead or simply wounded. He had no idea if any of them were because of him or not. He simply stayed by the colonel and fought on. He no longer felt tired; he was too numb. This was not how he had imagined a battle would be; this was slaughter.

The British were somehow on the move again, but the rebels paced them, harassing them continually with gunfire. With each rise in the road, more militia seemed to materialize from the trees, pouring fresh shots into the fray. The British weren't firing back as much now, and Joshua realized it was because they were running low on ammunition. They hadn't expected to meet this scale of rebellion, and failed to bring enough powder and shot to keep going. Joshua wondered if they would surrender, or fight on till they were all dead. Joshua wasn't sure how much more of this he could stomach.

Then, for some odd reason, the British began cheering. Joshua couldn't imagine why at first, until the report reached Colonel Barrett that English reinforcements had arrived. In the distance, Joshua heard a dull booming.

"They have cannon," the colonel explained. "It will not be so easy now. We had better rest here, boys. We've driven the English far enough and taken enough glory for ourselves. Let some of those who are fresher share it now." As his men started to collapse where they stood, Barrett beckoned Joshua over. "You've done well this day, Mister Havens," he said. Joshua swelled with pride at the praise. "Now, I think it due time that you be employed for the purpose you volunteered. I will gather all the information about this day's events that I can, and write you a letter to Ben Franklin. Make your way back to Concord for your horse, and then take the letter as swiftly as you can to the Continental Congress."

The colonel paused and looked all around. There were bodies littering the road, some still moving and groaning with pain. The red coats of the British were brighter red now with their lifeblood. "This day," he said, "we have lit the fire of freedom. It is a large fire, set on a hill, shedding its light over all the countryside. The British will never be able to hide its flames. It is burning, bright and clear. These brave men about us have begun something that will endure forever. Independence will come, and the light of this day will blaze the way."

Joshua, proud to have been a very small part of this beginning, felt light-headed at these words. "Amen," he said solemnly. "With God's help, this is but a brave start."

"Aye," Barrett agreed. "I know of none braver. People will speak of this day for a long time to come. It is the birth of a new nation, under God, and in the sight of the whole world. Tyranny shall not long endure!"

Chapter Nineteen

The sky was starting to darken, and Thomas was beginning to become impatient. Had Robert been telling the truth about the Vigilance Committee? Or had the warning been a false one, meant to worry Sarah and get some measure of revenge that way? Maybe Robert had gone back and told his father what he had done, changing the plans to attack on some other night? Questions flittered through his mind like the night moths in the fields. There were no answers to the questions, except that Thomas felt sure that Robert had not lied to them.

Thomas was ready and waiting, and so were all of the others. He wished that Mother had taken charge, but she had refused this post. While he appreciated her faith in him, Thomas wished she had chosen some other time and event to show her trust. Right now, he just wanted to fall into the background. Well, he *had* been the one who wanted to go to war, after all — and now he was at war, after a very strange fashion.

Everything looked perfectly normal around the farm — which had taken some careful planning. They didn't want to scare off the Vigilance Committee — yet. This had to be a lesson that they would never forget.

Thomas hoped it would not be a disaster that *he* would never forget.

He heard low voices, and saw, in the gloom, several people approaching. Excitement silenced his worries for the moment. The attack was obviously still on. Thomas briefly hoped that Robert had found some excuse to remain out of this, because he didn't want to hurt the other boy. Sarah might not marry him, but Thomas was certain she'd take a dim view of matters if he was hurt.

There were eight of them coming. Thomas could just make them out. Each had sticks or other wooden weapons in their hands, and one or two were laughing as they moved forward. Thomas swallowed, summoning all of his courage. Then he stepped out of hiding from behind the large tree, and uncovered his lantern.

The men were surprised, and jumped. Thomas took a few seconds to survey them; it gave him the time to force himself to speak. He recognized Mr. Rankine, and Mr. Allison, Robert's father. Daniel Allison was there also, and Benjamin Doyle. The other four faces he recognized, but could not put names to them. Robert, thankfully, was not with them.

"Is there something I can do for you, gentlemen?" he asked. He was astonished at how even and calm his voice was. "It's a little late for a social call, I'm afraid, and we have no food laid out for you."

"It's not food we're after," Mr. Rankine growled. "But there is indeed something you can do for us. We're here to teach you rebellious upstarts a lesson."

"I wasn't aware you'd taken up the profession of schoolteacher," Thomas answered. "I can see, though, that it isn't Scripture you're here to teach. As it says in the book of Proverbs: 'The evil bow before the good, and the wicked at the gates of the righteous.'" Thomas felt rather proud of himself for that one. "You're at our gates," he pointed out.

"And you are not welcome any further with sticks in your hands and hatred in your hearts."

"I'll not stand here to be mocked by a mere boy," Mr. Doyle snarled. "It's clear that the family is in severe need of that lesson we had planned. Come, lads, let's start by thrashing this one's hide."

"I would strongly advise you against it," Thomas warned them. "This is our land, by anyone's law you care for, and we will not allow anyone to invade it."

"I'll settle him," Daniel vowed, moving forward and raising the ax handle he carried.

Thomas raised the lantern and waved it. A couple of the men were smart enough to realize that this must be a signal, but the others were still muttering curses and threats and hurried forward. Thomas moved back behind the tree.

The twins, screaming wildly and clattering sticks against cooking pots, charged from the woods. In front of them, they drove the pigs, squealing and wild with fright. The pigs didn't care where they went, as long as they got away from the howling demons on their heels. They plowed into the Vigilance Committee, snorting and rumbling, scattering the men to either side of the path. The pigs didn't stop, of course, but kept right on running.

Thomas wasn't worried; they would calm down soon, and return to their run. They never went far from their food. The twins turned and bolted back toward the house, however.

The eight men were shaken by this, but more annoyed than hurt. Thomas hadn't expected the attack to do more than break their spirits a little. One of the men was limping, though, where a pig had trampled his foot, and another had been sent sprawling and lost his stick.

"This is your last chance to leave," Thomas warned them, stepping out from behind the tree again.

"Do you think one small trick can dampen our resolve?" Mr. Allison called. He brandished his stick. "You'll have broken bones for this, I swear!"

"On your own heads be it," Thomas said. "Literally."

He reached back to the tree as they came closer. With the butcher knife from the kitchen, he cut through the hemp rope, which was pulled taut behind the bole of the tree. With a crash, the branches overhead parted.

The attackers halted, and yelped as the open bottles crashed down. A couple of them failed to break, but most hit their targets, scattering their contents over the men and then injuring them again as the thin glass shattered. The strong, sweet smell of maple syrup filled the evening air.

"Now!" Thomas yelled loudly.

Mother and Sarah stepped out from their hiding places. Each carried a hornet's nest, and each wore protective clothing to prevent herself from being stung. With yells of their own, they heaved the nests at the committee members. Sarah's aim was a little off, and her nest slammed into the ground, shattering there. Mother's, however, was absolutely dead on, and the nest slammed into Mr. Allison's chest and burst.

Angry swarms of hornets rose like clouds from both wreckages, and settled their anger on the closest, sweetest targets — the eight intruders. Howling, the men flailed at their minute attackers, unable to shake them free. They had dropped their weapons, which were useless against the hornets, and were trying to clear the stinging monsters from their bodies. Thomas could not feel any sympathy for their agonies.

The twins had returned again, staying well back of the angry swarms, and they had emptied two jars of oil behind the flailing, cursing men. As soon as they dodged away again, Thomas took the bow and arrow from behind his tree. He lit an oil-soaked arrow at his lantern and fired it at the pool as the men, retreating and batting at their attackers, reached it.

The spilled oil there ignited, sending a jet of flame into the air. The men screamed again, as they narrowly avoided being caught in the blast. "Run!" Thomas jeered. "Run, and don't come back! If you do, the next time we shall not be so lenient with you! This is Havens land, and we bow to no tyrants — neither English nor loyalist! And if we can fight back, so can every good man and true in town. You may as well disband, because nobody will be afraid of you now!"

As the men limped off, Mother and Sarah moved out of hiding to join him. Then the twins, too, came running over, whooping and yowling quite as badly as if they had been born Indians. Thomas couldn't blame them for their enthusiasm. All of their attackers would be left stiff and sore, and would have to take long baths to remove the sticky syrup residue from themselves. Thomas doubted they would live past the shame of everyone knowing what had happened to them. And none would dare show their faces in town for days, until the hornets' stings had subsided.

"You did well, Thomas," Mother said approvingly.

"No," Thomas said, daring to contradict her. "*We* did well, all of us. This is Havens land, and we all defended it."

"Yes," Mother agreed. "We all did well. I'm very proud of my family, every last member of it. Even the pigs!"

Thomas went to get one of the leather buckets of water that they had placed ready. They couldn't allow the fires to burn unchecked — the flames might spread and damage the land. Sarah joined him, and together they doused the fires. Thomas felt a strange affection and respect for his sister.

Then, with a howl, something erupted from the trees and leaped upon him, sending Thomas sprawling on the ground. His head hit the earth, leaving him slightly dazed. But not so much so that he couldn't recognize his attacker. It was Daniel Allison, his face twisted and swollen from rage almost as much as from the stings he had suffered.

"You'll never beat an Allison!" Daniel screamed, raising his stick to brain Thomas with it. Thomas struggled to move, and only managed to raise an arm to block the coming blow. He was too stunned from hitting the ground to be able to defend himself properly.

With a scream of rage, Sarah whirled her leather bucket around her head and brought it crashing down onto Daniel's wrist. Daniel howled in pain, dropping his stick and clutching his hand. He backed off slightly, and Thomas caught his breath at last and managed to scramble to his feet to go to his sister's aid.

She didn't need it. She whirled the bucket around again and crashed it into Daniel's ribs. The breath was knocked from the older boy, and he fell to the ground, wheezing, tears streaming down his blistered face. Sarah yelled wordlessly, and kicked him hard in the ribs. Daniel didn't have the breath to scream, though he clearly wanted to do so. Sarah wasn't done with him, but Thomas suddenly felt sorry for the poor wretch. He caught his sister and pulled her back.

"Let me go," she snarled. "I want to beat the stuffing out of him!"

"You've already done it," Thomas informed her. Indeed, Daniel showed no inclination to get up off the ground. Thomas wasn't even sure the older boy could move. Sarah might have broken bones with either the blows or the kick.

Sarah calmed down slightly, though she was still panting angrily. With even more respect, Thomas smiled at his sister. "If he tries anything else, I promise you can break both his legs," he told her. Then he looked down at the whimpering Daniel.

"Have you had enough yet?" he asked. "Or shall I let this mere girl finish you off? It would look fine on your grave's headboard to say that a girl had placed you there."

"I'll go," Daniel promised. All of the arrogance appeared to have been beaten out of him.

"Smart decision," Thomas approved. He stepped back. Daniel clambered up slowly and painfully to his feet and then hobbled off. Thomas placed an arm about his sister's shoulders. "You know, I'm really glad that you're my sister. And I'm even more glad that you've never lost your temper like that with me!"

Sarah had calmed down, and managed to grin back. "Well, now you know not to try my patience!"

Thomas discovered that he felt really good. "Let's go home," he said.

Chapter Twenty

$\mathcal{T}$hings settled back to normal. Thomas and Sarah worked hard together. The twins collected the pigs the following morning, praising them and feeding them extra treats of spoiled vegetables. And probably one or two that weren't spoiled, too. The Vigilance Committee vanished, hiding their wounds and humiliation. The Allisons weren't at church on Sunday — and neither were six others.

And then Joshua returned, though very briefly. Thomas was helping Sarah bring the apples to the small shed where they had their cider press when they heard the rider coming. At first Thomas was afraid it was more trouble, but then he recognized Joshua on Freya. He and Sarah hollered their greetings as Joshua reined in beside them. Their brother looked tired but elated.

"I cannot stop," he apologized. "But I had to look

in as I passed. I'm bearing messages for Mister Franklin from Boston. The fighting has begun, and begun well. The British fired on our men, and we fired back."

Thomas looked at his brother with respect. "You were there, part of it?" he asked, proudly.

Joshua nodded. "I don't know how much help I was, but I was there at the start of it. We forced the British back. They rallied, but the day was ours. Our struggle for independence from the Crown has truly begun. Our commander said that we have lit a beacon for all the world to see, and freedom's fire is burning too brightly ever to be extinguished."

"I'm sure it is," Sarah said, just as proudly.

Joshua looked down from his seat at them both. "I am sorry that you had to stay home, Thomas," he apologized. "You're missing all of the action."

"Oh, I wouldn't say that." Thomas looked at Sarah, and they both laughed. He had never felt as close to his sister before. Nor had he felt so content. He didn't regret not being a soldier now. Mother had been right — this was where he should be, helping to look after his family, and to defend them. "Perhaps the time will come when I pick up a gun," he explained to Joshua. "But now, I know this is my place. I'm the man of the house, after all, and this house is where I should be."

"And we'd be lost without him," Sarah added affectionately. She was starting to lose her infatuation with Robert Allison. Thomas was sure she'd marry one day, and marry wisely. She had learned a lot in the past few days, and had matured. So had he, for that matter!

"You'd be breaking too many bones without me," he joked. They had heard that she'd snapped Daniel's wrist with her blow. So, it seemed, had half of the town. Daniel was not in evidence anywhere.

Joshua obviously didn't understand what they were talking about. "I wish I could say hello to Mother, but I have to press on. I'll be back as soon as I can, but I have work that must be done."

"We'll tell her you were here and are fine," Thomas promised. "Now, go, and do your job. And I'll remain here and do mine."

Joshua nodded and smiled down at them both. "God be with you all," he said, and then whirled Freya around. Setting his heels to her sides, he waved and then was off again.

"He seems happy enough," Sarah observed. "And, strangely, so do you."

"I feel happy," Thomas informed her. "I have learned that there are many ways to fight for freedom. Some do it with a musket." He grinned. "I do it with a hornet's nest!"

"And you do it well."

"Thank you." He looked at her. "And how about you? How happy are you?"

"I'm not sure," she admitted. "For the most part, fine. But then there are times when I think about Robert, and I feel like a bottomless well of tears. But it will pass; I know it will. There are other matters to occupy my heart." She looked down the trail. The dust from Freya's passing was already settling. "How long do you think it will be before this fight is over?"

Thomas shrugged. "I don't know. But I think it will not be over until we are free. None of us will let things stay the way they were. We'll fight to the end for our land and our right to do as we see fit. And we'll let no one stop us."

Sarah nodded. "Amen to that," she approved.

Bibliography

Several books proved useful to me while writing *Freedom's Fire*. Most notably:

Liberty! The American Revolution by Thomas Fleming (Viking, 1997)

Home Life in Colonial Days by Alice Morse Earle (Berkshire House Publishers, 1993, reprinting the original 1898 edition)

The Shot Heard 'Round The World, edited by Jeanne Munn Bracken (Discovery Enterprises, 1995)

I also visited the sites of the battles of Lexington and Concord, where the historic events are commemorated, and where many helpful people give tours of a number of the significant buildings that still stand as monuments to the founders of our liberty. I wish to express my appreciation to them all.

About the Author

J. P. Trent likes to wander around historical sites to soak up the vibes, and has visited castles, battle-fields, and strange standing stones in the United States and England. A native of Britannia, he now lives in one of the former thirteen Colonies. He has been known to write books under a variety of other identities.